18

JUNIOR CLASSICS

Published by
Rupa Publications India Pvt. Ltd 2016
7/16, Ansari Road, Daryaganj
New Delhi 110002

Sales centres:
Bengaluru Chennai
Hyderabad Jaipur Kathmandu
Kolkata Mumbai Prayagraj

This is a work of fiction. Names, characters, places and incidents are either the product of the author's imagination or are used fictitiously and any resemblance to any actual person, living or dead, events or locales is entirely coincidental.

P-ISBN: 978-81-291-3952-8
E-ISBN: 978-81-291-4417-1

Third impression 2023

10 9 8 7 6 5 4 3

Printed in India

Contents

The Adventure of the Creeping Man 4

The Adventure of the Illustrious Client 34

The Adventure of the Lion's Mane 64

The Adventure of the Mazarin Stone 94

The Adventure of the Creeping Man

Arthur Conan Doyle

Mr Holmes was always of the opinion that I should publish the facts connected with Professor Presbury, if only to dispel once and for all the ugly rumours which some twenty years ago agitated the university and were echoed in the learned societies of London. Due to certain obstacles, this curious case remained in the tin box which contains so many records of my friend's adventures. Now we have at last obtained permission to expose the facts which formed one of the very last cases handled by Holmes before his retirement from practice. Even now a certain discretion has to be observed in laying the matter before the public.

It was one Sunday evening early in September of the year 1903 that I received one of Holmes's precise messages:

The relations between us in those days were peculiar. He was a man of habits, narrow and concentrated habits, and I had become one of them. I was his whetstone, his comrade on whom he could bounce off his thoughts, and when I irritated him with a certain methodical slowness in my mentality, that irritation served only to make his own flame-like intuitions and impressions flash up more vividly and swiftly. Such was my humble role in our alliance.

When I arrived at Baker Street, he was in the throes of some annoying problem. For about half an hour he gave no sign that he was aware of my presence, then he seemed to come out of his reverie and greeted me with his usual whimsical smile.

'You will excuse a certain abstraction of mind, my dear Watson,' said he. 'Some curious facts have been submitted to me within the last twenty-four hours, and they in turn have given rise to some speculations of a more general character. I have serious thoughts of writing a small monograph upon the uses of dogs in the work of the detective. You may recollect that in the case which you, in your sensational way, coupled with the Copper Beeches, I was able, by watching the mind of the child, to form a deduction as to the criminal habits of the very smug and respectable father.'

'Yes, I remember it well.'

'My line of thoughts about dogs is similar. A dog reflects the family life. Who has ever seen a frisky dog in a gloomy family, or a sad dog in a happy one? Snarling people have snarling dogs, dangerous people have dangerous ones. And their passing moods may reflect the passing moods of others.'

I shook my head.

'Surely, Holmes, this is a little farfetched,' said I.

He had refilled his pipe and resumed his seat, taking no notice of my comment.

'The practical application of what I have said is very close to the problem which I am investigating. It is a tangled thread, you understand, and I am looking for a loose end. One possible loose end lies in the question: Why does Professor Presbury's wolfhound, Roy, attempt to bite him?'

I sank back in my chair with disappointment, thinking whether I was summoned from home for this trivial issue? Holmes glanced across at me.

'The same old Watson!' said he. 'You never learn that the gravest issues may depend upon the smallest things. But is it not strange that a staid, elderly philosopher—you've heard of Presbury, of course, the famous Camford physiologist—whose friend has been his devoted wolfhound, should now have been twice attacked by his own dog? What do you make of it?'

'The dog is ill.'

'Well, that has to be considered. But he attacks no one else, nor does he apparently molest his master, save on very special occasions. Curious, Watson—very curious.'

There was a quick step on the stairs, a sharp tap at the door, and a moment later the new client—Mr Bennett—presented himself. He was a tall, handsome man about thirty, well dressed and elegant, but with something in his bearing which suggested shyness. He shook hands with Holmes, and then looked with some surprise at me.

'This is a delicate matter, Mr Holmes, considering my relation with Professor Presbury, both personally and professionally. I can hardly discuss the matter in presence of a third person.'

'Have no fear, Mr Bennett. Dr Watson is the very soul of discretion, and I can assure you that this is a matter in which I am very likely to need an assistant.'

'As you like, Mr Holmes.'

'You will appreciate it, Watson, when I tell you that this gentleman, Mr Trevor Bennett, is a professional assistant to the great scientist, lives under his roof, and is engaged to his only daughter. His devotion and loyalty to the professor make it important for him to clear this strange mystery.'

'I hope so, Mr Holmes. That is my one object. Does Dr Watson know the situation?'

'I have not had time to explain it.'

'Then perhaps, I had better go over the ground again before explaining some fresh developments.'

'I will do so myself,' said Holmes. 'The professor, Watson, is a man of European reputation. His life has been academic. There has never been a breath of scandal. He is a widower with one daughter, Edith. He is, I gather, a man of very energetic and positive qualities, one might almost say a combative character. So the matter stood until a very few months ago.

'Then the current of his life was broken. He is sixty-one years of age, but he became engaged to the daughter of Professor Morphy, his colleague in the chair of comparative anatomy. It did not meet with full approval of his own family. Professor Presbury was rich, however, and there was no objection upon the part of the father. The daughter, however, had other views, and there were already several candidates for her hand, who, if they were less eligible from a worldly point of view, were at least more of an age. The girl, Alice

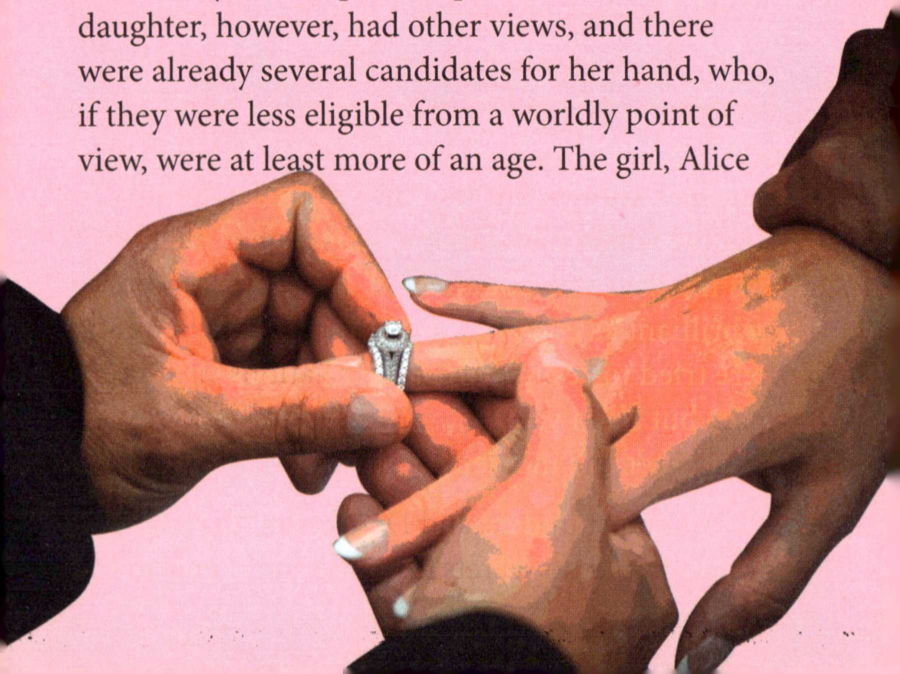

Morphy, seemed to like the professor too in spite of his eccentricities. Only the age stood in the way.

'About this time a little mystery appeared in the professor's life. He did what he had never done before. He left home and gave no indication where he was going. He was away for a fortnight and returned looking rather travel-worn. He made no mention of where he had been.

'It was by chance that Mr Bennett here, received a letter from a fellow student in Prague, who said that he was glad to have seen Professor Presbury there, although he had not been able to talk to him. Only then they came to know where he had been.

'Now comes the point. From that time onward a curious change came over the professor. He became furtive and sly. Those around him had always the feeling that he was not the man that they had known, but that he was under some shadow which had darkened his higher qualities. His intellect was not affected. His lectures were as brilliant as ever. His daughter and Mr Bennett here tried to resume their old relations with the man, but all in vain. Now Mr Bennett, tell in your own words the incident of the letters.'

'You must understand Dr Watson, that the professor had no secrets from me, and I enjoyed

his confidence like his own son. As his secretary, I handled all his mail. But shortly after his return, this changed. He told me that certain letters might come to him from London, which would be marked by a cross under the stamp. These were to be set aside for his own eyes only. I may say that several of these did pass through my hands, that they had the EC mark, and were in illegible handwriting. If he answered them at all the answers did not pass through my hands, nor into the letter-basket in which our correspondence was collected.'

'And the box,' said Holmes.

'Ah, yes, the box. The professor brought back a little wooden box from his travels. It was one of those quaint carved things which one associates with Germany. This he placed in his instrument cupboard. One day, in looking for a cannula, I took up the box. To my surprise he was very angry, and reproved me in very harsh words. I tried to explain that it was an accident but I could make out throughout the evening that he was angry with me. That was on July 2nd. On that very day, Roy attacked the professor as he came from his study into the hall. Again, on July 11th, there was a scene of the same sort, and then I have a note of yet another upon July 20th. After that we had to banish Roy to the stables.'

'Singular! Most singular!' Holmes murmured. 'These details were new to me, Mr Bennett, but you also spoke of some new developments.'

'What I speak of, occurred the night before last,' said he. 'I was lying awake about two in the morning, when I was aware of a dull muffled sound coming from the passage. I opened my door and peeped out. I should explain that the professor sleeps at the end of the passage—'

'The date being—?' asked Holmes.

Our visitor was clearly annoyed at so irrelevant an interruption, 'I have said, sir, that it was the night before last—that is, September 4th.'

Holmes nodded and smiled.

He continued, 'He sleeps at the end of the passage and would have to pass my door in order to reach the staircase. It was a really terrifying experience, Mr Holmes. I was shaken by what I saw. The passage was dark, save that one window halfway along it threw a patch of light.

'I could see that something was coming along the passage, something dark and crouching. Then suddenly it emerged into the light, and I saw that it was him. He was crawling, Mr Holmes—crawling! He was not quite on his hands and knees. I should rather say on his hands and feet, with his face sunk between his hands. Yet he seemed to move with ease. I was so paralyzed by the sight that it was not until he had reached my door that I was able to step forward and ask if I could assist him. His answer was extraordinary. He sprang up, spat out some atrocious word at me, and hurried on past me, and down the staircase. I waited about for an hour, but he did not come back. It must have been daylight before he regained his room.'

'Well, Watson, what make you of that?' asked Holmes.

'Lumbago, possibly. I have known a severe attack make a man walk in just such a way.'

'Good Watson! You always keep us rooted on ground, but we can hardly accept lumbago, since he was able to stand erect in a moment.'

'He was never in better health,' said Mr Bennett. 'In fact, he is stronger than I have ever seen him. Both Edith—Miss Presbury—and I feel this is not something we can watch passively, and that we are moving towards disaster, but we can't take it to the police.'

'It is certainly a very curious and suggestive case. What do you think, Watson?'

'Speaking as a medical man,' said I, 'it appears to be a case for an psychiatrist. The old gentleman's cerebral processes were disturbed by the love affair. He made a journey abroad in the hope of breaking himself of the passion. His letters and the box may be connected with some other private transaction.'

'And the wolfhound no doubt disapproved of the financial bargain. No, no, Watson, there is more in it than this. Now, I can only suggest—'

What Holmes was about to suggest was interrupted by a young lady shown into the room. As she appeared Mr Bennett sprang up with a cry and ran forward with his hands out to meet those which she had herself outstretched.

'Edith, dear! Nothing the matter, I hope?'

'I felt I must follow you. Oh, Jack, I have been so dreadfully frightened! It is awful to be there alone.'

Our new visitor, a bright, handsome girl of a conventional English type, smiled back at Holmes as she seated herself beside Mr Bennett.

'When I found Mr Bennett had left his hotel, I thought I should probably find him here. Of course, he had told me that he would consult you. But, oh, Mr Holmes, can you do nothing for my poor father?'

'I have hopes, Miss Presbury, but the case is still obscure. Perhaps what you have to say may throw some fresh light upon it.'

'It was last night, Mr Holmes. I was awakened by the dog barking most furiously. Poor Roy, he is chained now near the stable. My room is on the second floor. It happened that the blind was up in my window, and there was bright moonlight outside. As I lay with my eyes fixed upon the square of light, listening to the frenzied barkings of the dog, I was amazed to see my father's face looking in at me. Mr Holmes, I nearly died of

surprise and horror. There it was, pressed against the windowpane, and one hand seemed to be raised as if to push up the window. If that window had opened, I think I should have gone mad.

'It was no delusion, Mr Holmes. Don't deceive yourself by thinking so. I dare say it was twenty seconds or so that I lay paralyzed and watched the face. Then it vanished, but I could not—I could not spring out of bed and look out after it. I lay cold and shivering till morning. At breakfast he was sharp and fierce in manner, and made no reference to the adventure of the night. Neither did I, but I gave an excuse for coming to town—and here I am.'

Holmes looked thoroughly surprised at Miss Presbury's narrative.

'My dear young lady, you say that your room is on the second floor. Is there a long ladder in the garden?'

'No, Mr Holmes, that is the amazing part of it. There is no possible way of reaching the window—and yet he was there.'

'The date being September 5th,' said Holmes. 'That certainly complicates matters.'

It was the young lady's turn to look surprised.

'This is the second time that you have alluded to the date, Mr Holmes,' said Mr Bennett. 'Is it possible that it has any bearing upon the case?'

'It is possible—very possible—and yet I have not my full material at present.'

'Possibly you are thinking of the connection between insanity and phases of the moon?'

'No, I assure you. It was quite a different line of thought. Possibly you can leave your notebook with me, and I will check the dates. Now I think,

Watson, that our line of action is perfectly clear. This young lady has informed us that her father remembers little or nothing which occurs upon certain dates. We will therefore call upon him as if he had given us an appointment upon such a date. He will put it down to his own lack of memory. Thus we will open our campaign by having a good close view of him.'

'That is excellent,' said Mr Bennett. 'I warn you, however, that the professor is short-tempered and violent at times.'

Holmes smiled.

'There are reasons why we should come at once. Tomorrow, Mr Bennett, will certainly see us in Camford.'

Monday morning found us on our way to the famous university town. Holmes made no mention of the case until we reached our hotel.

'I think, Watson, that we can catch the professor just before lunch. He lectures at eleven and should have an interval at home.'

'What possible excuse have we for calling?'

Holmes glanced at his notebook. 'There was a period of excitement upon August 26th. We will assume that he is a little hazy as to what he does at such times. If we insist that we are there by appointment I think he will hardly venture to contradict us.'

'We can try.'

Shortly we pulled up at the door of a charming house, girt round with lawns and covered with purple wisteria. Professor Presbury was certainly surrounded with every sign not only of comfort, but of luxury. Even as we pulled up, a grizzled head appeared at the front window, and we were aware of a pair of keen eyes from under shaggy brows which surveyed us through large horn glasses. A moment later we were actually in his sanctum, and the mysterious scientist, whose actions had brought us from London, was standing before us. There was certainly no sign of eccentricity, either in his manner or appearance, for he was a portly, large-featured man, grave, tall and frock-coated, with the dignity of bearing which a lecturer needs. His eyes were his most remarkable feature, keen, observant and clever to the verge of cunning.

He looked at our cards.

'Pray sit down, gentlemen. What can I do for you?'

Mr Holmes smiled amiably. 'It was the question which I was about to put to you, Professor.'

'To me, sir!'

'Possibly there is some mistake. I heard through a second person that Professor Presbury of Camford had need of my services.'

'Oh, indeed!'

It seemed to me that there was a malicious sparkle in the intense gray eyes.

'You heard that, did you? May I ask the name of your informant?'

'I am sorry, Professor, but the matter was rather confidential. If I have made a mistake there is no harm done. I can only express my regret.'

'Not at all. I should wish to go further into this matter. It interests me. Have you any scrap of writing, any letter or telegram, to bear out your assertion?'

'No, I have not.'

'I presume that you do not go so far as to assert that I summoned you?'

'I would rather answer no questions,' said Holmes.

'No, I dare say not,' said the professor sharply. 'However, that particular one can be answered very easily without your aid.'

He walked across the room to the bell. Mr Bennett answered the call.

'Come in, Mr Bennett. These two gentlemen have come from London under the impression that they have been summoned. You handle all my correspondence. Have you a note of anything going to a person named Holmes?'

'No, sir,' Bennett answered with a flush.

'That is conclusive,' said the professor, glaring angrily at my companion. 'Now, sir'—he leaned forward with his two hands upon the table—'it seems to me that your position is a very questionable one.'

Holmes shrugged his shoulders.

'I can only repeat that I am sorry that we have made a needless intrusion.'

'Hardly enough, Mr Holmes!' he said in a screaming tone.

He got between us and the door as he spoke, and he shook his two hands at us with furious passion.

'You can hardly get out of it so easily as that.'

His face was convulsed, and he grinned and gibbered at us in his senseless rage. I am convinced that we should have had to fight our way out of the room if Mr Bennett had not intervened.

'My dear Professor,' he cried, 'consider your position! Consider the scandal at the university! Mr Holmes is a well-known man. You cannot possibly treat him with such discourtesy.'

Sulkily our host—if I may call him so—cleared the path to the door. We found ourselves outside the door. Holmes seemed greatly amused. There were the sounds of running feet behind, but it was, to my relief, not the formidable professor but his assistant who appeared round the curve of the drive. He came panting up to us.

'I am so sorry, Mr Holmes. I wished to apologize.'

'My dear sir, there is no need. It is all in the way of professional experience.'

'I have never seen him in a more dangerous mood. But he grows more frightening. You can understand now why his daughter and I are alarmed. And yet his mind is perfectly clear.'

'Too clear!' said Holmes. 'That was my miscalculation. It is evident that his memory is much more reliable than I had thought. By the way, can we, before we go, see the window of Miss Presbury's room?'

Mr Bennett pushed his way through some shrubs, and we had a view of the side of the house.

'It is there. The second on the left.'

'Dear me, it seems hardly accessible. And yet

you will observe that there is a creeper below and a water pipe above which can give some foothold.'

'I could not climb it myself,' said Mr Bennett. 'There was one other thing I wish to tell you, Mr Holmes. I have the address of the man in London to whom the professor writes.'

Holmes glanced at the paper and put it into his pocket.

'Dorak—a curious name. Slavonic, I imagine. Well, it is an important link in the chain. We return to London this afternoon, Mr Bennett. I see no good purpose to be served by our remaining. We cannot arrest the professor because he has committed no crime, nor can we place him under constraint, for he cannot be proved to be mad. No action is as yet possible.'

'Then what on earth are we to do?'

'A little patience, Mr Bennett. Things will soon develop. Unless I am mistaken, next Tuesday may mark a crisis. Certainly we shall be in Camford on that day. And if Miss Presbury can prolong her visit—'

'That should be easy.'

'Then let her stay till we can assure her that all danger is past. Meanwhile let him have his way, as long as he is in good mood there is no problem.'

Just then we saw the tall figure of the professor emerging from the house. Mr Bennett quickly waved goodbye and joined his employer and they both went inside, having what seemed to be an animated and excited conversation.

'I expect the professor put two and two together, and he came across as having a particularly clear and logical brain from the little I saw of him. Our friend Mr Bennett might face some uncomfortable time.'

Holmes stopped at a post office and sent off a telegram on our way. The answer reached us in the evening, and he tossed it across to me.

> Have visited the Commercial Road and seen Dorak. Suave person, bohemian, elderly. Keeps large general store.
> —Mercer.

Mercer is my general utility man who does routine work for me. Now we know little about the man with whom the professor was secretly corresponding. The nationality of the person also connects with his Prague visit.

'Thank goodness that something connects with something,' said I. 'At present we seem to be faced by a long series of inexplicable incidents with no bearing upon each other.'

'Well, now, let us take the dates first,' said he, his fingertips together and his manner as if he were addressing a class.

'This excellent young man's diary shows that there was trouble upon July 2nd, and from then onward it seems to have been at nine day intervals, with, so far as I remember, only one exception. Thus the last outbreak upon Friday was on September 3rd, which also falls into the series, as did August 26th, which preceded it. The thing is beyond coincidence.'

I was forced to agree.

'Let us, then, form the provisional theory that every nine days the professor takes some strong drug which has a passing but highly poisonous effect. His naturally violent nature is intensified by it. He learned to take this drug while he was in Prague, and is now supplied to him by a bohemian middleman in London.'

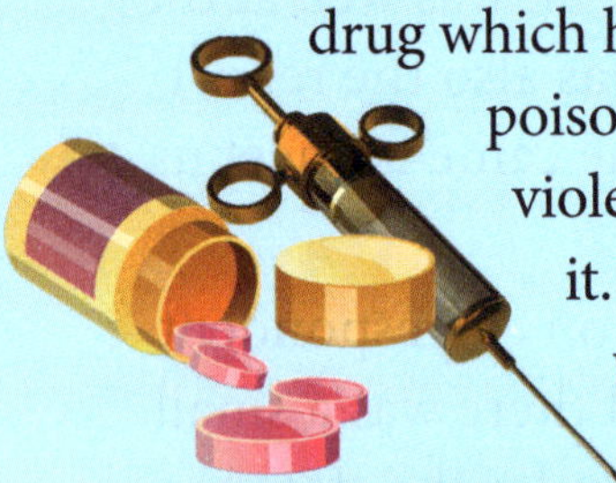

'But the dog, the face at the window, the creeping man in the passage?'

'Well, well, we have made a beginning. I should not expect any fresh developments until next Tuesday. In the meantime we can only keep in touch with friend Bennett and enjoy the amenities of this charming town.'

In the morning Mr Bennett slipped round to bring us the latest report. As Holmes expected, Mr Bennett had some uneasy time with the professor. He was rough and rude but this morning he was himself again and delivered brilliant lecture to his class. Apart from fits, he never had more energy or vitality or his brain clearer than now, but he is not the same man.

'I don't think you have anything to fear now for a week at least,' Holmes answered. 'Let us agree that we meet here at this hour next Tuesday. Meanwhile, keep us posted in what occurs.'

I didn't see much of my friend till next Tuesday when he explained to me on the train as we travelled to Camford that all was well at the professor's residence. This was also the report given by Mr Bennett when he came to meet us at the hotel in the evening.

'He heard from his London correspondent today. There was a letter and there was a small packet, each with the cross under the stamp, which warned me not to touch them. There has been nothing else.'

'That may prove quite enough,' said Holmes. 'We might reach to some conclusion tonight if my deductions are correct. It is necessary to hold the professor under observation. I would suggest, you remain awake and should you hear him pass your door, follow him as discreetly as you can. We will not be far off. Where is the key to that little box you spoke?'

'Upon his watch-chain.'

'We will need to have a look at it. Have you any other able-bodied man on the premises?'

'There is the coachman, Macphail.'

'Where does he sleep?'

'Over the stables.'

'We might possibly want him. Well, we can do no more until we see how things develop. Goodbye, but I expect that we shall see you before morning.'

We took our positions by midnight among the bushes right opposite the professor's hall door.

'If the cycle of nine days holds good, then we shall have the professor at his worst tonight,' said Holmes. 'The fact that these strange symptoms began after his visit to Prague, his secret correspondence and the packet he receives periodically, show that he takes something under definitive directions which regulate his behaviour. Have you noted his knuckles? Thick and hornlike in a way I have never seen before.'

Just then the hall door opened and professor stepped out. He was erect with arms dangling but as he moved forward on the sidewalk, he crouched and moved on his hands and feet. He skipped sometimes, as if he had an overflow of energy. As he disappeared around the corner, Mr Bennett was seen following him quietly.

'Come Watson', said Holmes.

We moved out of the bushes and took a place where we could see outside of the house. The professor was crouching at the foot of the ivy plant covering the wall, and in a second, he started climbing it with great agility, jumping from branch to branch, as if just for enjoyment. He then climbed down and moved towards the stable. The wolfhound was barking madly and straining on his chain. The professor, in a strange manner, started provoking the dog with sticks and pebbles. And then in a moment the dog's collar slipped and he had the professor by the throat. We could hear growls and screams. Before we could reach them, the professor was senseless. Mr Bennett's voice brought the dog under control.

The dog was chained again, and together we carried the professor inside, where I, along with help of Mr Bennett, dressed his wounded throat. The teeth had passed very close to a main artery and the bleeding was heavy, but in half an hour, the danger was past. I gave him a morphia injection and he slept peacefully. I suggested that a surgeon should see professor but Mr Bennett refused,

saying as of now this secret was within the family, and if it went out, it might affect his position in the University and hurt his daughter's feelings too.

'It is quite possible to keep the matters to ourselves' Holmes said. 'Let us check the box and see what we find in it.'

Inside was an empty phial, a used syringe, and some invoices written in foreign hand. The marks on the envelopes showed that they were those which had disturbed the routine of the secretary, and each was dated from the Commercial Road and signed 'A Dorak'. They were mere invoices to say that a fresh bottle was being sent to Professor Presbury, or receipt to acknowledge money. There was one other envelope, however, bearing the Austrian stamp with the postmark of Prague.

'Here we have our material!' cried Holmes as he tore out the enclosure.

Honoured Colleague [it ran]:

Since your esteemed visit I have thought much of your case, and though in your circumstances there are some special reasons for the treatment, I would nonetheless warn you, as my results have shown that it is not without danger of a kind. I have, as I explained to you, used black-faced langur because a specimen was accessible. Langur is, of course, a crawler and climber, while anthropoid walks erect and is in all ways nearer. I beg you

to take every possible precaution that there be no premature revelation of the process. I have one other client in England, and Dorak is my agent for both. Weekly reports will oblige. —Yours with high esteem, H Lowenstein.

Lowenstein! The name brought back to me the memory of some snippet from a newspaper, which spoke of an obscure scientist who was striving in some unknown way for the secret of the elixir of life. Lowenstein of Prague! Lowenstein with the wondrous strength-giving serum, tabooed by the profession because he refused to reveal its source. In a few words I said what I remembered. Mr Bennett had taken a manual of zoology from the shelves.

'Langur,' he read, 'the great black-faced monkey of the Himalayan slopes, biggest and most human of climbing monkeys. Well, thanks to you, Mr Holmes, it is very clear that we have traced the evil to its source.'

'The real source,' said Holmes, 'lies, of course, in that untimely love affair which gave our careless professor the idea that he could only gain his wish by turning himself into a younger man.'

He sat musing for a little with the phial in his hand, looking at the clear liquid within.

'When I have written to this man and told him that I hold him criminally responsible for the poisons which he circulates, we will have no more trouble. But it may recur. Others may find a better way. There is danger there—a very real danger to humanity.'

Suddenly the dreamer disappeared, and Holmes, the man of action, sprang from his chair.

'I think there is nothing more to be said, Mr Bennett. The various incidents will now fit themselves easily into the general scheme. The dog, of course, was aware of the change far more quickly than you. His smell would insure that. It was the monkey, not the professor, whom Roy attacked, just as it was the monkey who teased Roy. Climbing was a joy to the creature, and it was a mere chance, I take it, that the pastime brought him to the young lady's window. There is an early train to town, Watson, but I think we shall just have time for a cup of tea at the Chequers before we catch it.'

The Adventure
of the
Illustrious Client
Arthur Conan Doyle

On the upper floor of the Northumberland Avenue establishment there is an isolated corner where two couches lie side by side, and it was on these that we lay upon 3 September 1902, the day when my narrative begins. I had asked

Sherlock Holmes whether anything was stirring, and for answer he had shot his long, thin, nervous arm out of the sheets which enveloped him and had drawn an envelope from the inside pocket of the coat which hung beside him.

It was from the Carlton Club and dated the evening before. This is what I read:

Sir James Damery presents his compliments to Mr Sherlock Holmes and will call upon him at 4:30 tomorrow. Sir James begs to say that the matter upon which he desires to consult Mr Holmes is very delicate and also very important. He trusts, therefore, that Mr Holmes will make every effort to grant this interview and that he will confirm it over the telephone to the Carlton Club.

'I need not say that I have confirmed it, Watson,' said Holmes as I returned the paper. 'Do you know anything of this man Damery?'

'Only that this name is a household word in society. He has rather a reputation for arranging delicate matters which are to be kept out of the papers. You may remember his negotiations with Sir George Lewis over the Hammerford Will case. He is a man of the world with a natural turn of diplomacy. I am bound, therefore, to hope that it is not a false scent and that he has some real need for our assistance.'

'Ours?'

'Well, if you will be so good, Watson.'

'I shall be honoured.'

'Then we have the hour—4:30.'

Sharp to the half hour, Colonel Sir James Damery was announced. Many will remember that honest personality, clean-shaven face and that pleasant mellow voice.

'Of course, I was prepared to find Dr Watson,' he remarked with the courteous bow. 'His collaboration may be very necessary, for we are dealing on this occasion, Mr Holmes, with a man to whom violence is familiar and who will, literally, stick at nothing. I should say that there is no dangerous man in Europe.'

'May I ask his name?' said Mr Holmes.

'Have you ever heard of Baron Gruner?'

'You mean the Austrian murderer?'

Colonel Damery threw up his hands with a laugh.

'There is no getting past you, Mr Holmes! Wonderful! So you have already sized him up as a murderer?'

'It is my business to follow the details of continental crime. It was a purely technical legal point and the suspicious death of a witness that saved him: I am sure that he killed his wife when the so-called "accident" happened in the Splügen

Pass as if I had seen him do it. Well, what has Baron Gruner been up to? I presume it is not this old tragedy which has come up again?'

'No, it is more serious than that. To revenge crime is important, but to prevent it is more so. I am sure you will sympathize with the client in whose interest I am acting.'

'Who is the client?'

'Mr Holmes, surely the actual name of your client is immaterial.'

'I am sorry,' said Mr Holmes. 'I am accustomed to have mystery at one end of my cases, but to have it at both the ends is too confusing. I fear, Sir James, that I must decline to act.'

Our visitor was greatly disturbed. His large, sensitive face was darkened with emotion and disappointment.

'You hardly realize the effect of your own action, Mr Holmes,' said he. 'You place me in a most serious dilemma, for I am perfectly certain that you would be proud to take over the case if I could give you the facts, and yet a promise forbids me from revealing them all. He is General de Merville. He has a daughter, Violet de Merville, a

young, rich, beautiful, accomplished, a wonder-woman in every way. It is this daughter, this lovely, innocent girl, whom we are endeavoring to save from the clutches of a friend.'

'Baron Gruner has some hold over her, then?'

'The strongest of all holds where a woman is concerned—the hold of love. The fellow is extraordinarily handsome, with a most fascinating manner, a gentle voice, and that air of romance and mystery which means so much to a woman. He is said to have the whole female gender at his mercy and to have made ample use of the fact.'

'But how come such a man met a lady of the standing of Miss Violet de Merville?'

'It was on a Mediterranean yachting voyage. The villain attached himself to the lady, and with such effect that he has completely and absolutely won her heart. She dotes upon him, she is obsessed by him. She will not hear one word against him. To sum up, she proposes to marry him next month. As she is of age and a will of iron, it is hard to know how to prevent her.'

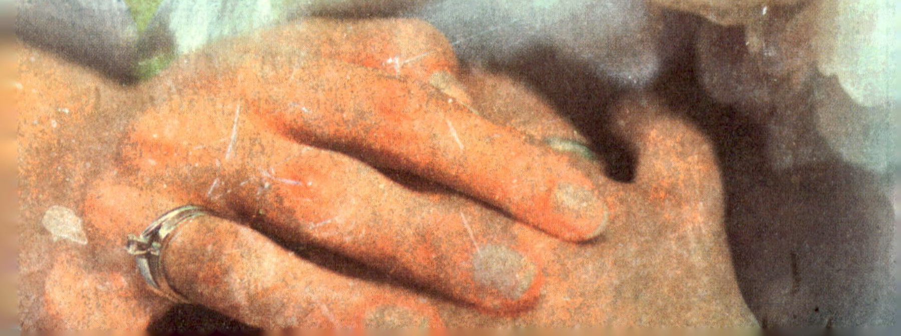

'Does she knows about the Austrian episode?'

'The cunning devil has told her about every public scandal of his past life, but always in such a way as to make himself out to be an innocent martyr. She absolutely accepts his version and will listen to no other.'

'Dear me! But surely you have inadvertently let out the name of your client? It is no doubt General de Merville.'

Our visitor fidgeted in his chair.

'I could deceive you by saying so, Mr Holmes, but it would not be true. De Merville is a broken man. He has lost the nerve which never failed him on the battlefield and has become a weak, doddering old man, utterly incapable of contending with a brilliant, forceful rascal like this Austrian. My client, however, is an old friend, one who has known the General intimately for many years and taken a paternal interest in this young girl since she wore short frocks. He cannot see this tragedy fulfill itself without some attempt to stop it. There is nothing on which Scotland Yard can act. It was his own suggestion that you should be called in, but it was, as I have said, on condition that he should not be personally involved in the matter. I request you to keep my client's name secret.'

'I promise that,' said Mr Holmes, 'your problems interest me, and I shall be prepared to look into it. How shall I keep in touch with you?'

'The Carlton Club will find me. But in case of emergency, there is a private telephone call, "XX.31."'

'The Baron's present address, please?'

'Vernon lodge, near Kingston. It is a large house. He is a rich man, which naturally makes him a more dangerous opponent.'

'Is he at home at present?'

'Yes.'

'Can you give any further information about the man?'

'He has expensive tastes. He is a horse fancier. For a short time he played polo at Hurlingham, but then this Prague affair got noised about and he had to leave. He collects books and pictures. He is a man with a considerable artistic side of his nature. He is a recognized authority on Chinese pottery and has written a book upon this subject.'

'A complex mind,' said Mr Holmes. 'All great criminals have that. Well, Sir James, you will

inform your client that I am turning my mind upon Baron Gruner. I have some sources of information of my own, and I dare say we may find some means of opening the matter up.'

When our visitor had left, Holmes sat long in deep thought, however, he came briskly back to earth.

'Well, Watson, any views?' he asked.

'I should think you better see the young lady herself.'

'My dear Watson, if her poor old broken father cannot move her, how shall I, a stranger, prevail? I think we must begin from a different angle. I rather fancy that Shinwell Johnson might be a help.'

I have not had the occasion to mention Shinwell Johnson in these memoirs because I have seldom drawn my cases from the latter phases of my friend's career. During the first years of the century he became a valuable assistant. Johnson made his name first as very dangerous villain and server of two terms at Parkhurst. Finally he repented and allied himself to Holmes, acting as his agent in the huge criminal underworld of London and obtaining information of importance. It was to him that Sherlock Holmes now proposed to turn.

It was not possible for me to follow the immediate steps taken by my friend, for I had some pressing professional business of my own, but I met him by appointment that evening at Simpson's, where, sitting at a small table in the front window and looking down at the rushing stream of life in the Strand, he told me something of what had passed.

'Johnson is on the prowl,' said he. 'He may pick up some garbage in the darker recesses of the underworld, for it is down there, amid the black roots of crime, that we must hunt for this man's secrets.'

'But if the lady will not accept what is already known, why should any fresh discovery of yours turn her from her purpose?'

'Oh, to be sure, I had not told you of my plans. When I had given Johnson his instructions, I took a cab out to Kingston and found the Baron in an friendly mood.'

'Did he recognize you?'

'Yes, for I sent in my card.'

'You say he was friendly?'

'Some people's friendliness is more deadly than the violence of coarser souls. His greeting was characteristic. "I thought, I should see you sooner or later, Mr Holmes," said he. "You have been engaged, no doubt by General de Merville, to stop my marriage with his daughter, Violet. Is it not?"

'I agreed.'

'"My dear man," said he, "you will only ruin your own well-deserved reputation. You cannot possibly succeed. Let me advise you to draw off at once."

"It is curious," I answered, "but that was the very advice which I had intended to give you. Surely you would be wiser if you left the lady alone. It would not be pleasant for you if the facts of your past were brought to her notice."

'The Baron finally broke into a gentle chuckle.'

"Excuse my amusement, Mr Holmes. Let me make the thing clear to you, I have been fortunate enough to win the entire affection of this lady in spite of the facts I told her very clearly of all the unhappy incidents in my past life. I also told her that some wicked people would come to her and tell her these things and I warned her how to treat them. You have heard of post-hypnotic suggestion, Mr Holmes? Well you will see how it works."

'Well, Watson, there seemed to be no more to say, so I took my leave but he stopped me.'

"By the way Mr Holmes," said he, "did you know Le Brun, the French agent?"

"Yes," I said.

"Do you know what befell him?"

"I heard that he was beaten by some Apaches in the Montmartre district and crippled for life."

"Quite true, Mr Holmes, he had been enquiring into my affairs. Don't do it. My last word to you is go your own way and let me go mine. Goodbye."

'So there you are, Watson. You are up-to-date now.'

'The fellow seems dangerous. Must you interfere? Does it really matter if he marries the girl?'

'Well, well, we need not discuss that, come home with me, for Shinwell will be there with his report.'

We found him sure enough. Besides him on the settee was a slim, beautiful young woman with a pale, intense face, youthful, yet so worn with sorrow.

'This is Miss Kitty Winter,' said Shinwell Johnson. 'She will speak for herself.'

'If I can help to put him where he belongs, I am yours to the end,' the woman said, with an intense hatred on her face.

'What I am, Adelbert Gruner made me. Oh, if I could only pull him into the pit where he has pushed so many! Gruner is after some other poor fool and wants to marry her and you want to stop it.'

'She is not in her senses. She is madly in love.'

'Told about the murder?'

'Yes.'

'Couldn't you lay proofs before her silly eyes?'

'Well, can you help us do so?'

'Am I not a proof myself? If I stood before her and told her how he used me...'

'Would you do this?'

'Would I?'

'Well, it might be worth trying. But he has told her most of his sins and had pardon from her.'

'I'll say he didn't tell her all,' said Miss Winter. 'I caught a glimpse of one or two murders. He has a book—a brown leather book with a lock, and his arms in gold on the outside. I think he was a bit drunk that night, or he would not have shown it

to me. Mr Holmes, this man collects women and takes pride in his collection. He had photographs, names, details everything about them in that book.'

'Where is it?'

'May be it is still in the pigeon-hole of the old bureau in the inner study. Do you know his house?'

'I've been in the study,' said Mr Holmes.

'Have you? The outer study is the one with a Chinese crockery in it. Then behind his desk is the door that leads to the inner study—a small room where he keeps papers and things.'

'Is he not afraid of burglars?'

'There is a burglar alarm at night.'

'Well, now Miss Winter,' said Holmes, 'if you would call here tomorrow evening at five, I would consider in the meanwhile whether your

suggestion of seeing this lady personally may be arranged. I am exceedingly obliged to you for your co-operation. My clients will consider liberally.'

'None of that, Mr Holmes,' cried the young woman. 'I am not out of money. Let me see this man in the mud. That's my price.'

***

I did not see Holmes again until the following evening when we dined once more at our Strand restaurant. He shrugged his shoulders when I asked him what luck he had had in his interview.

'There was no difficulty at all about the appointment,' said Holmes. 'The General phoned that all was according to schedule at 104 Berkeley Square where the lady was awaiting us. She knew what we had come for. Miss Winter's arrival rather amazed her.

"Well, sir," said Miss de Merville, "you have called, as I understand, to malign my fiancé Baron Gruner. It is only by my father's request that I see you and I warn you in advance that anything you can say would not possible have the slightest effect upon my mind."

'I was sorry for her, Watson. I really did plead with her. I spared her nothing—the shame, the fear, the agony, the hopelessness of it all I thought of what the rascal had said about a post-hypnotic influence.

"I have listened to you with patience, Mr Holmes," said Miss de Merville. "I am aware that Adelbert, my fiancé, had a stormy life in which he has incurred bitter hatred and most unjust attack on his reputation. I learn that you are a paid agent who would have been willing to act for the Baron as against him. I wish you to understand once for all that I love him and that he loves me."

'She turned towards my companion and said, "Who is this young lady?"

"I'll tell you who I am," she shouted, springing out of her chair, her mouth all twisted with passion. "I am his last mistress. I am one of a hundred that he has tempted, used, ruined and thrown into the refuse heap, as he will do with you also. I tell you foolish woman, if you marry this man he'll be the death of you."

"I should prefer not discuss such matters," said Miss de Merville coldly.

"You fool! You unutterable fool!"

"Mr Holmes, I beg that you will bring this interview to an end. I have obeyed my father's wish in seeing you, but I am not forced to listen to the ravings of this person."

'Miss Winter darted forward

to clutch her hair. I dragged her towards the door and was lucky to get her back into the cab without a public scene.

'Watson, so now once again you exactly know how we stand and it is clear that I must plan some fresh opening move, for this trick won't work. I'll keep in touch with you.'

The London Chronicle: OR, UNIVERSAL EVENING POST.

***

It was between the Grand Hotel and Charing Cross Station, where a news vendor displayed his evening papers. The date was just two days after the last conversation. The news was terrible—Murderous Attack upon Sherlock Holmes. I stood stunned for some moments. Then I snatched a paper from the man whom I had not paid, and turned up the fateful paragraph. This was how it ran:

'We learn that Mr Sherlock Holmes, the well-known private detective was the victim this morning of a murderous assault which had left him in an insecure position. Mr Holmes was beaten about the head and body, receiving injuries which the doctors describe as most serious. He was carried to Charing Cross Hospital and afterwards insisted upon begin taken to his room in Baker Street. The miscreants who attacked him belonged to the criminal fraternity.'

I sprung into horse drawn cab and was on my way to Baker Street. I found Sir Leslic Oakshott, the famous surgeon.

'No immediate danger,' was his report. 'Two lacerated scalp wounds and some bruises. Several stitches have been necessary. Morphine has been injected. An interview of a few minutes is permitted.'

I sat beside Holmes and bent my head.

'All right, Watson, don't look so scared,' he muttered in a very weak voice. 'It's not as bad as it seems.'

'Thank God for that! What can I do, Holmes? I'll go and thrash them.'

'Good old Watson! No, we can do nothing there unless the police lay their hands on the men. I have my plans. The first thing is to exaggerate my injuries.'

'But Sir Leslic Oakshott.'

'I'll look after that.'

'Anything else?'

'Yes, tell Shinwell Johnson to get Miss Winter out of the way. They will be after her now as they know that she was with me in the case. That is urgent. Do it tonight.'

I arranged with Johnson that evening to take Miss Winter to a quiet suburb and see that she lay low until the danger was past. For six days the public were under the impression that Holmes was at the door of death. My continual visits assured me that it was not so bad as that this determined will was working wonders. He was recovering fast. On the seventh day the stitches were taken out, in spite of which there was a report of infection producing inflammation is the evening papers. The same evening papers had an announcement that among the passengers on the boat *Ruritania*, starting from Liverpool on Friday, was Baron Adelbert Gruner, who had some important

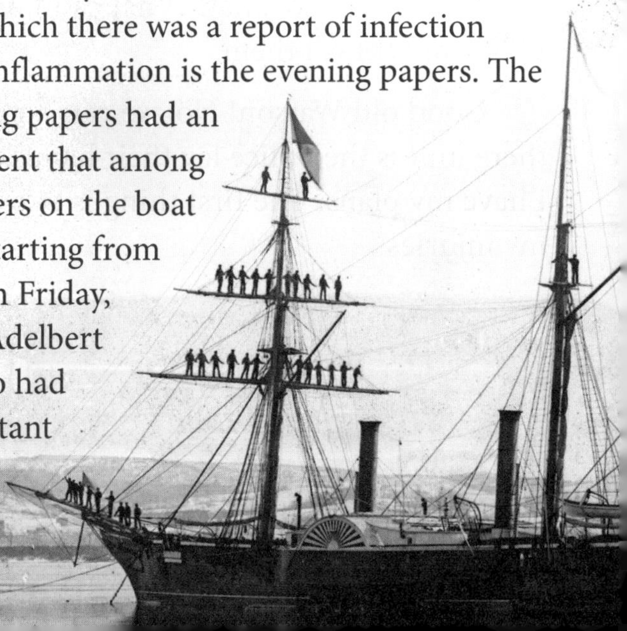

financial business to settle in the states before his wedding to Miss Violet de Merville.

'Friday!' cried Holmes. 'Only three days. I believe he wants to keep out of danger. But he won't, Watson, and I want you to spend the next twenty-four hours in an intensive study of Chinese pottery.'

He gave no explanation and I asked for none. I drove to the London Library in St James Square and carried a big volume to my room. All that evening and all that night. I was sucking in knowledge and memorizing names. With all the information I called upon Holmes next evening. He was out of bed now.

'Why, Holmes,' I said, 'if one believed the papers you are dying.'

'That,' said he, 'is the impression which I intended to convey Watson, have you learned your lessons?'

'I have tried to.'

'Good, you could keep up an intelligent conversation on the subject?'

Holmes opened the lid of a little box and took out a small object carefully wrapped in some fine Eastern silk. He unfolded and disclosed a delicate little saucer of deep-blue colour.

'This is the real egg-shell pottery of the Ming dynasty. A complete set of this would be worth a king's ransom.'

'What am I to do with it?'

Holmes handed me a card upon which was printed: 'Dr Hill Barton, 369 Half Moon Street'.

'That is your name for the evening, Watson. You will call upon Baron Gruner and say that you are bringing him a specimen of an absolutely unique set of Ming China. You may as well be a doctor. You are a collector and this set has come your way. You have heard of the Baron's interest in the subject and you are not opposed to selling at a price.'

'I would perhaps suggest that the set should be valued by an expert.'

'Excellent, Watson, you talk cleverly today.'

On the same evening, with the precious saucer in my hand and the card of Dr Hill Barton in my pocket, I set off on my own adventure. The beautiful house indicated that Baron Gruner was a man of considerable wealth. A butler showed me in and a plush-clad footman ushered me into the Baron's presence.

'Pray sit down, Doctor,' said he. 'Have you the Ming saucer with you of which you spoke?'

I carefully unpacked it and handed it to him. He pulled over the lamp to examine it. He was certainly a remarkably handsome man. His voice was engaging and his manners perfect. In age he looked a little over thirty, though his record showed that he was forty-two.

'Very fine—very fine indeed!' he said at last. 'What puzzles me is that I only know of one in England to match this and it is certainly not likely to be in the market. Dr Hill Barton, how did you obtain this?'

'Does it really matter? You can see that the piece is genuine.'

'That the piece is genuine is certain but suppose it would prove afterwards that you had no right to sell?'

'I would guarantee you against any claim of the sort.'

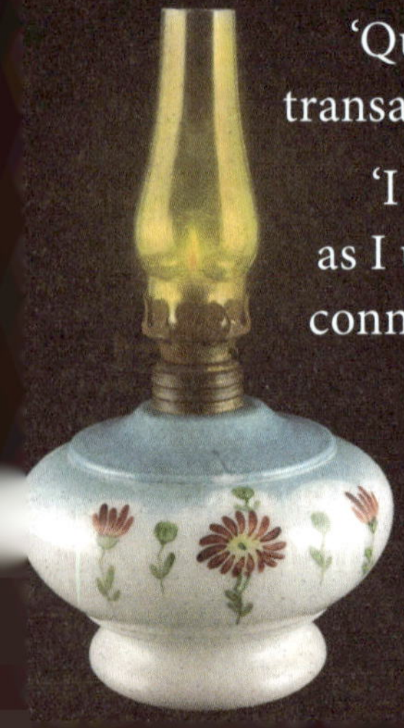

'Quite so, and yet the whole transaction strikes me as rather unusual.'

'I have given you the first offer as I understood that you were a connoisseur.'

'Who told you I was a connoisseur?'

'I was aware that you had written a book upon the subject.'

'Have you read the book?'

'No, I am a busy man. I am a doctor in practice.'

'That is no answer. If a man has a hobby he follows it up no matter how busy. Might I ask you a few questions to test you? Whether you are a connoisseur? Tell me a little about the Northern Wei dynasty and the place in the history of ceramics. What do you know about Emperor Shomu?'

'This is intolerable, sir,' said I. 'I come here to do you a favour and not to be examined as if I were a school boy. I certainly shall not answer questions which have been put in so offensive a way.'

'What is the game? You are here as a spy. You are on a mission of Holmes. This is a trick you are playing upon me. You will find hard to get out of here.'

He almost jumped on his feet, dived his hand into a side drawer and searched violently. Then something struck his ear, for he stood listening intently and ran into the room behind him. The window leading out to the garden was wide open. Beside it, looking like some terrible ghost, his head with bloody bandages, his face drawn and white, stood Sherlock Holmes.

The next moment I heard the crash of his body among the laurel bushes outside. The master of the house rushed after him to the open window. And then it was done in an instant. I clearly saw it. An arm—a woman's arm—shot out from among the leaves and immediately the Baron uttered a horrible cry. He clapped his two hands on his face and rushed round the room, beating his head horribly against the walls. Then he fell on the carpet, rolling and writhing and screaming.

'Water! For God's sake, water!' was his cry.

The acid was eating into his face everywhere and dripping from the ears and the chin. The features which I had admired a few minutes before were disfigured because of the acid attack.

'It was that hell-cat Kitty Winter!' he cried. 'Oh, the she-devil! She shall pay for it!'

I bathed his face in oil, put soft cotton material on the raw surface and administered a morphine injection. I was relieved when his family surgeon, closely followed by a specialist came to relieve me of my charge. An inspector of police had also arrived and to him I handed my real card. Then I left the house of gloom and terror and within an hour was at Baker Street.

Holmes was shocked by the events of the evening and he listened with horror to my account of the Baron's transformation.

'Here is the book the woman talked of. If this will not break off the wedding, nothing ever could. It will Watson. It must. No self-respecting woman would stand it.'

'Is it his love diary?'

'Call it what you will. The moment the woman told us about the book, I realized what a good weapon was there if we could lay our hands on it. I would have waited a little longer but the Baron's visit to America forced me change my plan. Burglary at night is impossible. But there was a chance in the evening if I could only be sure that his attention was engaged. That was where you and your blue saucer came in. I had only a few minutes to act. Therefore I took the girl at the last moment. How would I guess what the little packet was that she carried under cloak?

'He guessed I came from you.'

'I feared he would. But you held him in play just long enough for me to get the book, though not long enough for an unobserved escape. Ah, Sir James, I am very glad you have come!'

Our courtly friend had appeared in answer to a previous summons. He listened with the deepest attention to Holmes's account of what had occurred.

'You have done wonders—wonders!' he cried when he had heard the narrative. 'But if these injuries are as terrible as Dr Watson describes, then surely our purpose of thwarting the marriage is sufficiently gained without the use of this horrible book.'

Holmes shook his head.

'Women of the De Merville type do not act like that. She would love him the more as a disfigured martyr. No, no. It is his moral side, not his physical, which we have to destroy. That book will bring her back to earth—and I know nothing else that could. It is in his own writing. She cannot get past it.'

Sir James carried away both it and the precious saucer. As I was myself overdue, I went down with him into the street. A carriage was waiting for him. He sprang in, gave a hurried order to the coachman, and drove swiftly away. He flung his overcoat half out of the window to cover the coat of arms upon the panel, but I had seen them in the glare of our fanlight none the less. I gasped with surprise. Then I turned back and ascended the stairs to Holmes's room.

'I have found out who our client is,' I cried, bursting with my great news. 'Why, Holmes, it is—'

'It is a loyal friend and a chivalrous gentleman,' said Holmes, holding up a restraining hand. 'Let that now and forever be enough for us.'

I do not know how the incriminating book was used. Sir James may have managed it. Or it is more probable that so delicate a task was entrusted to the young lady's father.

The effect, at any rate, was all that could be desired. Three days later appeared a paragraph in the *Morning Post* to say that the wedding between Baron Adelbert Gruner and Miss Violet de Merville would not take place.

The same paper had the first court hearing of the proceedings against Miss Kitty Winter on the grave charge of vitriol-throwing. Such relieving circumstances came out in the trial that the sentence, as will be remembered, was the lowest that was possible for such an offence. Holmes was threatened with a prosecution for burglary, but when an object is good and a client is sufficiently illustrious, even the rigid British law becomes human and elastic. My friend has not yet stood in the dock.

The Adventure of the Lion's Mane
Arthur Conan Doyle

The unique thing about this problem, which was just as complex as any that I faced during my long career, was that it came to me after my retirement. I had settled down in Sussex, enjoying the natural life for which I yearned during the long years spent in London and that's where it occurred.

By this time, Watson had gone his way too and we hardly met. Thus it is that I must tell this story myself showing by my words each step upon the difficult road which lay before me as I searched for the mystery of the Lion's Mane.

My villa stood on the southern slope of the downs, with a great view of the Channel. All around me were chalk cliffs and the only passage to the coastline below was by a pathway that was steep and slippery. At the bottom was a stretch of pebbles and shingle, with curves and hollows here and there, which would fill up with each flow of the tide and served as swimming pools. The beach stretched in both directions and in between was the village and cove of Fulworth.

Half a mile away from my house was Harold Stackhurst's famous coaching academy, The Gables, where students prepared for various professions and teachers who helped them. Stackhurst and I were good friends and would often spend time together.

Towards the end of July 1907, there was a severe storm that left a lagoon at the base of the cliff after the tide receded. Next morning, the wind had slowed down and the surroundings were washed and fresh, so I decided to take a walk before breakfast to enjoy the scenery. As I walked along the cliff path, I heard a cheery voice calling my name, and turned to find Harold Stackhurst, who was apparently out for a swim. We exchanged pleasantries and it came out that McPherson had preceded him and they were to meet at the lagoon.

Fitzroy McPherson was the science master at the academy. A natural athlete he was excellent in every game that did not require physical strain as he had had heart trouble following rheumatic fever. He was a keen swimmer and we often went swimming together.

At this moment we saw McPherson. First his head showed up above the cliff edge, where the pathway ends, and then his body came into view. He was staggering like a man drunk. Suddenly he threw up his hands and with a terrible cry; fell on his face. Stackhurst and I rushed to him and turned him on his back. He was obviously dying. He regained consciousness for a moment, and he uttered a few words as if warning us. They were indistinct, but I could make out the last few; which came out almost in a shriek and those were 'the Lion's Mane'. It was meaningless and hard to understand and yet I could not attribute it to any other sense. Then he half raised himself from the ground and fell forward on his side. He was dead.

My companion was horrified at the sight, but my senses were alert. McPherson was dressed only in his Burberry overcoat, his trousers and an unlaced pair of canvas shoes. As he fell over, his overcoat fell from his shoulders, his body was exposed. His back was covered with dark red lines as though he had been flogged by a thin wire whip. The punishment-inflicting instrument seemed to be flexible for the marks curved round his shoulders and ribs. There was blood on his chin, for he had bitten through his lower lip in his agony.

I was kneeling and Stackhurst standing by the body when a shadow fell across us, and we found that Ian Murdoch had joined us. Murdoch was the mathematics coach at the academy a tall, dark, thin man, so reserved and aloof by nature that he had almost no friends. He seemed to live in his own world and had negligible connection with ordinary life. He was considered odd by the students, but none dared to upset him as there was a strange air

about him and he was known to have a ferocious temper. On one occasion, being irritated by McPherson's little dog he had picked up the animal and threw it through the window. Stackhurst would have dismissed him for that act, but he was a very good teacher. Such was the strange complex man who now appeared beside us. He seemed to be honestly shocked at the sight, though the incident of the dog might indicate that there was no friendship between the dead man and himself.

'Poor fellow! What can I do? How can help?'

'Were you with him? Can you tell us what has happened?'

'No, I was late this morning. I was not on the beach. I have come straight from The Gables. What can I do?'

'You can hurry to the police station at Fulworth and report the matter.'

Without another word, he walked away quickly and I turned to the matter in hand while Stackhurst remained by the body. My first task obviously was to note who was on the beach. From the top of the path, the whole beach was visible and it was deserted. Two or three people could be seen in the distance, moving towards Fulworth village. I walked down the path. The ground beneath was soft and I noticed the same footstep, going up and down. No one else had used the track that morning, to go to the beach. At one place I saw the print of an open hand with the fingers towards the incline. This meant that McPherson had fallen as he came up. There were rounded depressions, too, which suggested that he had come down on his knees several times. At the bottom, was the lagoon left by the retreating tide. McPherson had undressed at its side, for his towel lay on a rock. It was unused, so it seemed that he had never entered the water. As I hunted around on the ground, I noticed the prints of his canvas shoes and also of his barefeet. The latter fact showed that he had prepared to bathe, though the towel indicated that he had not actually done so.

Here, then, was the problem—as strange as any I had ever faced. The man had not been on the beach more than a quarter of an hour at the most. Stackhurst followed him and that confirmed the fact. He had gone to bathe and had stripped, as the bare footsteps showed. Then he had suddenly dressed again—they were all in disarray and open—and he had returned without bathing or at least without drying himself. The reason for this change of mind had been that he was hurt in some savage inhuman way, to the extent that he bit through his lower lip in agony and had just enough strength left to crawl away and die. Who had done this ghastly act? There were some small caves and covered places in the base of the cliffs, but they were lit up by sunlight and there was no place to hide. As for the distant figures on the beach, they seemed too far away to be connected. On the sea were two or three fishing boats. Their occupants might be examined later.

When I returned to the body, I saw that Ian Murdoch had arrived with Anderson, the village constable. He listened to everything and finally drew me aside.

'What's your advice, Mr Holmes, this is a big thing for me and I can't afford to go wrong.'

I advised him to call his superior and a doctor, also to allow nothing to be moved until they came. Then I searched the dead man's pockets. There were his handkerchief, a large knife and a small card-case, from which projected a slip of paper. This I unfolded and handed it to the constable. On it was a scrawled message in feminine hand:

I will be there, you may be sure.—Maudie.

The constable replaced everything in the pockets of the overcoat. I walked back to my house for breakfast, after arranging that the base of the cliffs should be thoroughly searched. Stackhurst came around to inform me that the body had been removed to The Gables and that nothing had been found in the small caves below the cliff. He had examined McPherson's desk and there were several notes which indicated intimate correspondence with a certain Miss Maud Bellamy, of Fulworth.

He explained, 'There is no doubt that it was a serious love affair, but there is no reason to connect it with the horrible incident except that she had made an appointment with him.'

'But why at a bathing pool that all of you used,' I remarked.

He said, 'By chance, the students were not with McPherson, Ian Murdoch kept them back for some algebraic demonstration before breakfast. He is sorry about it.'

'But yet they were not friends.'

'Earlier they were not, but lately, Muroch had been very close to McPherson. He is not of a very social nature'.

'What about the ill-treatment of a dog?'

'That was settled, I am sure they were real friends.'

'Do you know the girl?'

'Everyone knows her. She is the local beauty. McPherson was attracted to her, but I had no idea that things had gone so far as the letters indicate.'

'Who is she?'

'She is the daughter of Tom Bellamy, who owns all the boats and bathing-cots at Fulworth. He and his son William run the business.'

'Shall we visit them?'

'On what pretext?'

'We can easily do that. This fellow did not inflict the injuries upon himself. Someone else used the whip, if it was a whip that caused the injuries. His friends here were surely limited. Let us follow all trails to come to the motive and thereby to the criminal.'

As we approached the village, we noticed that several modern houses had been built upon the rising ground, behind the old-fashioned hamlet.

Stackhurst guided me, 'That is Haven, the Bellamy house. The one with the corner tower and slate roof. Look at that!'

The gate of The Haven had opened and Ian Murdoch, the mathematician, emerged. We came face to face on the road.

The man nodded and would have passed us but Stackhurst held him back.

'What were you doing there?' he asked.

Murdoch answered angrily, 'I am your subordinate at the academy, but not answerable towards my private doings.'

Stackhurst lost his temper, 'You are being insulting.'

'Your question is too.'

'You have done it earlier too but this is certainly the last, kindly make arrangements for your future elsewhere at the earliest.'

'It was intended. I have lost my only friend at The Gables, so it's not for me anymore.'

With that, he went away.

The first thing that stuck me was that Murdoch was finding an escape route. We went forward to the house of Bellamys.

Mr Bellamy was a middle-aged man. He seemed to be in a very angry mood.

'No, sir, I do not need any explanations. My son'—pointing to a strong young man, with a heavy sullen face, in the corner of the sitting room—'has the same opinion as me that Mr McPherson's affair with Maud was insulting. There were letters and meetings and much more without any intention of marriage and this we cannot approve. She has no mother and we are her only guardians. We are determined.'

He stopped speaking as the lady herself appeared. She would easily fit into any gathering of beautiful females, undoubtedly. Women have seldom been an attraction to me, for my brain has always governed my heart but one look at her face and it was apparent that no young man would pass her without a second look. Such was the girl who came through the door and stood in front of Stackhurst, wide-eyed and intense.

'I know that Fitzroy is dead,' she said. 'Do tell me the specifics.'

'This other friend of yours let us know the news,' explained the father.

'There is no reason that my sister should be involved in this matter,' growled the younger man.

The sister gave him a sharp look.

'This is my business, William. Please let me handle it. A crime has been committed. If I can help to show who did it, it is the least I can do for him who is gone.'

She listened to a short account from my friend with a concentration that showed that she possessed strong character along with great beauty. It seems that she already knew me, for she turned to me at the end.

'Bring them to justice, Mr Holmes, whoever they may be. I will help you along.'

She appeared to glance defiantly at her father and brother as she spoke.

'Thank you,' said I. 'I value a woman's instinct in such matters. You use the word "they". You think that more than one was involved?'

'I knew Mr McPherson was a brave and strong man. No single person could have inflicted such injuries upon him.'

'May I have a word with you alone?'

'I tell you, Maud, not to mix yourself up in the matter,' said her father angrily.

She looked at me helplessly.

'Everyone will know the facts in time, so there is no harm if I discuss them here,' said I. 'I should have preferred privacy but if your father disagrees then he can share the discussions.'

Then I spoke of the note that had been found in the dead man's pocket.

'It is sure to be produced at the inquest. Can you tell us something about it?'

'I see no reason for mystery,' she answered. 'We were engaged to be married and we only kept it secret because Fitzroy's uncle, who is very old and dying, might have disinherited him if he married against his wish.'

'You could have told us,' growled Mr Bellamy.

'So I would, father, if you had shown sympathy.'

'I object to my girl picking up with men outside her own kind.'

'It was your dislike of him that prevented us from telling you. As to this appointment'—she produced a crumpled note from her dress—'it was in answer to this.'

Dearest: The old place on the beach just after sunset on Tuesday. It is the only time I can get away.—FM

'Tuesday was today and I had meant to meet him tonight.'

I turned over the paper.

'This never came by post. How did you get it?'

'I would rather not answer that question. It has no relevance to the matter under investigation, but anything connected with the matter. I will readily answer.'

She kept her word, but there was nothing that helped the investigation. She had no reasons to think that her fiancé had any hidden enemy, but she admitted that she had several admirers.

'May I ask if Mr Ian Murdoch was one of them?'

She blushed and seemed confused.

'There was a time when I thought he was. But it changed when he understood the relations between Fitzroy and myself.'

Again our suspicions against this strange man seemed to be getting stronger. His rooms must be privately searched and his record examined. Stackhurst agreed to collaborate. We returned from our visit to The Haven with the hope that a beginning had been made.

A week passed. The inquest did not reveal anything pertaining to the matter and was postponed till further evidence. Stackhurst had inquired about his subordinate and had even searched his room, but without result. Personally, I had gone over the whole ground again, physically and mentally, but with no new conclusions. For the first time ever, even my imagination could find no solution to the mystery. Then there came the incident of the dog.

It was my old housekeeper who heard of it first.

'Sad story this, sir, about Mr McPherson's dog,' she said one evening.

'What of Mr McPherson's dog?'

'Dead, sir. Died of grief for its master.'

'Who told you this?'

'Why, sir, everyone is talking about it. Did not eat anything for a week. Then today two students from The Gables found it dead—down on the beach, sir, at the very place where its master met his end.'

'At the very place.'

The words stuck in my memory. My mind said it was vital. The dog's death was according to the beautiful faithful nature of dogs but 'in the very place' was it possible that it also had been sacrificed to some revengeful feud? Yes, it seemed possible in my mind. Shortly I was on my way to The Gables, where I found Stackhurst in his study. At my request he sent for the two students who had found the dog.

'Yes, it lay on the very edge of the pool,' said one of them. 'It must have followed the trail of its dead master. I saw the faithful little creature, laid out upon the mat in the hall. The body was stiff and rigid, the eyes projecting and the limbs contorted. There must have been great agony, it was apparent.'

From The Gables I walked down to the bathing pool. The sun had sunk and the shadow of the cliff lay black across the water. The place was deserted and there was no sign of life except for two sea birds circling and screaming overhead. For a long time I stood in deep thought while the shadows grew darker around me. At last, I turned and walked slowly homeward.

I had just reached the top of the path when it came to me. I remembered the thing for which I had been searching. As Watson has written earlier, I hold a vast store of knowledge without any system, but readily available for the needs of my work. I had known that there was something related to this matter. It was still vague but at least I knew how I could make it clear.

There is a great attic in my house, which is stuffed with books. It was into this that I entered and looked around for an hour. At the end of that time, I came out with a little book. I looked up the chapter of which I had a dim remembrance. It was late when

I retired, with my mind eagerly anticipating the work that was to be done tomorrow.

I had hardly finished my early cup of tea and was leaving for the beach when I had a call from Inspector Bardle of the Sussex police, 'I know your immense experience, sir,' said he. 'I am worried about this McPherson case. The worry is that should I make an arrest or not?'

'Meaning, Mr Ian Murdoch?'

'Yes, sir. There is really no one else when you come to think of it. If he did not do it, then who did?'

'What do you have against him?'

He had thought along the same lines as I had. There was Murdoch's character and the mystery which seemed to hang around him. His bursts of furious temper, as shown in the incident of the dog. The fact that he had a fight with McPherson earlier and there was reason to think that he might have resented his relationship with Miss Bellamy.

'What would my position be if I let him slip away with all this evidence against him?'

The big man was troubled in his mind.

I said, 'Consider all the gaps in your case. On the morning of the crime he can easily prove an alibi. He had been with his students till the last moment and within a few minutes of McPherson's

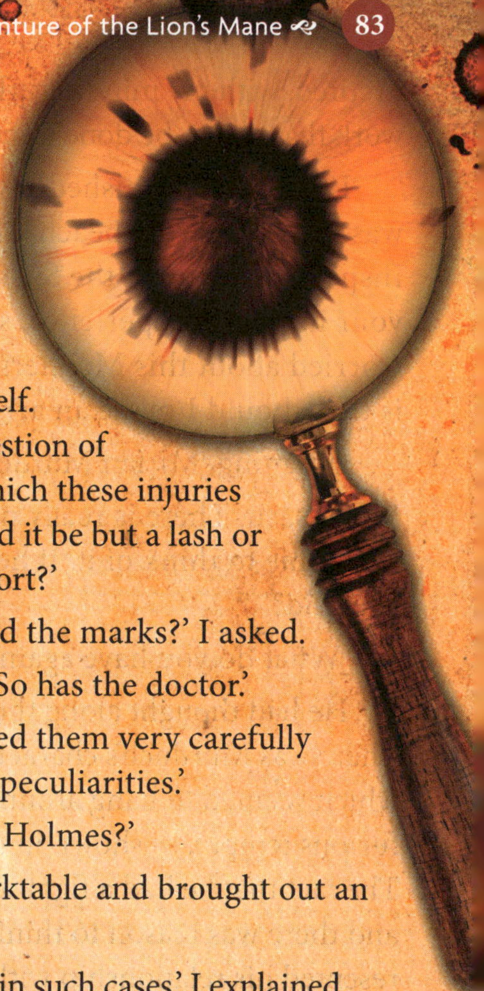

appearance, he came upon us from behind. Then keep in mind the absolute impossibility that he alone could have inflicted this kind of injury upon a man quite as strong as himself. Finally there is this question of the instrument with which these injuries were caused: what could it be but a lash or flexible whip of some sort?'

'Have you examined the marks?' I asked.

'I have seen them. So has the doctor.'

'But I have examined them very carefully with a lens. They have peculiarities.'

'What are they, Mr Holmes?'

I walked to my worktable and brought out an enlarged photograph.

'This is my method in such cases,' I explained. 'Now let us consider this weal which extends round the right shoulder. Do you see nothing remarkable?'

'I can't say I do.'

'Surely it is evident that it is unequal in its intensity. There is a dot of blood here and another there. There are similar indications in this other weal down here. What can that mean?'

'I have no idea. Have you?'

'I may be able to say more soon. Anything which will define what made that mark will bring us a long way towards the criminal.'

'By God, Mr Holmes, I think you have hit it.'

'Or there may be some very different cause, Mr Bardle. But your case is far too weak for an arrest. Besides, we have those last words— "the Lion's Mane".'

'I have wondered whether Ian—'

'Yes, I have considered that. If the second word had borne any resemblance to Murdoch— but it did not. He almost shouted it. I am sure that it was "Mane".'

'Have you no alternative, Mr Holmes?'

'Maybe I have, but I do not care to discuss it until there is something more solid.'

'And when will that be?'

'In an hour—possibly less.'

The inspector rubbed his chin and looked at me uncertainly. 'Perhaps it's those fishing boats.'

'No, no, they were too far out.'

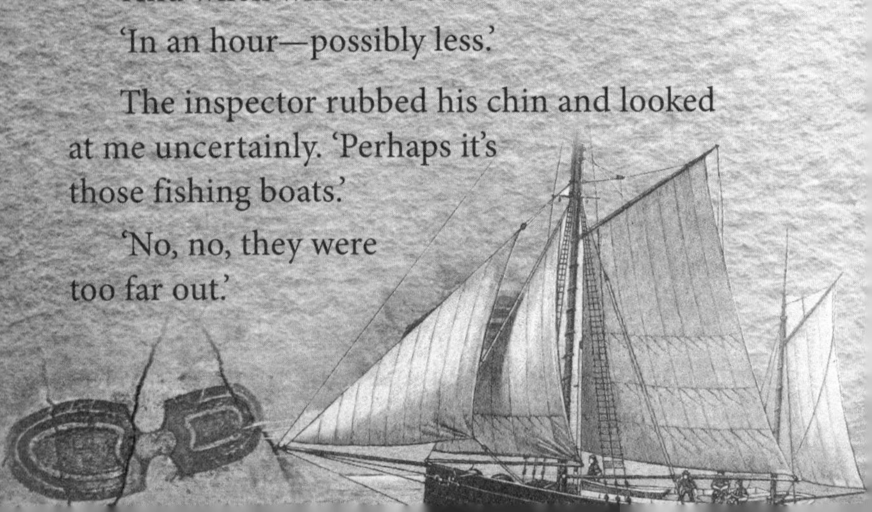

'Well, then, is it Bellamy and that big son of his?'

They were not very fond of Mr McPherson. Could they have done him harm?

'No, you won't draw me until I am ready,' I said with a smile.

'Now, Inspector, we each have our own work to do. Perhaps if you were to meet me here at midday.'

At this point we were interrupted. My outer door was thrown open, there were blundering footsteps in the passage and Ian Murdoch staggered into the room—pale, his clothes in disorder, taking help of the furniture to hold himself erect.

'Brandy! Brandy!' he gasped and fell groaning on the sofa.

Behind him came Stackhurst, hatless and panting, almost as bewildered as his companion.

'Yes, brandy!' he cried. 'The man is almost dead. It took all my effort to get him here, he fainted twice in the way.'

Half a glass of brandy brought a change. He pushed himself up and removed his coat from his shoulder.

'Oil, opium, morphine!' he cried. 'Anything to ease this terrible agony!'

The inspector and I were shocked at the sight. There, crisscrossed upon the man's exposed shoulder, was the same strange pattern of red

swollen line which had been the death mark of Fitzroy McPherson.

It was evident that pain was unbearable. The man's breathing would stop for a while, his face would turn black and then gasping he would hold his heart with his hand, sweating heavily. More and more brandy was poured down his throat, each fresh dose bringing him back to life. Pads of cotton wool soaked in salad oil seemed to ease the agony of the strange wounds. At last, his head fell heavily upon the cushion. He was half sleep and half faint, but apparently the pain had lessened.

It was not possible to question him but the moment we were assured of his condition, Stackhurst turned upon me.

'What is it, Holmes?' he cried.

'Where did you find him?' I asked.

'Down on the beach. Exactly where McPherson met his end. If this man's heart had been weak as McPherson's he would not be here now. More than once I thought he was gone as I brought him up.'

'Did you see him on the beach?'

'I was walking on the cliff when I heard his cry. He was at the edge of the water, staggering like a drunken man. I ran down, put some clothes on him and brought him up. Can you, with your worldwide reputation, do nothing for us?'

'I think I can, Stackhurst. Come with me now. And you, Inspector, come along. We will see if we cannot deliver this murderer into your hands.'

Leaving the unconscious man with the housekeeper, the three of us went down to the deadly lagoon. Slowly I walked round the edge of the water. The pool was mostly shallow but at the base of the cliff, it was four or five feet deep. It was the part favoured by swimmers. A line of rocks lay above it and along this I led the way, peering into the depths beneath me. I had reached the deepest and stillest part when my eyes saw what they were searching and I burst into a triumphant shout

'Cyanea!' I cried. 'Behold the Lion's Mane!'

The strange object at which I pointed did indeed look like a tangled mass torn from the mane of a lion. It lay on a rocky shelf about three feet under the water—a curious waving, vibrating, hairy creature with streaks of silver among its yellow hair.

I said, 'Help me Stackhurst!'

There was a big boulder just above the ledge and we pushed it down into the water. We saw that it had settled upon the ledge below. One flapping edge of yellow membrane showed that our victim was beneath it.

'What was it, Mr Holmes?' asked the

inspector, 'I belong here, but I never saw such a thing. It's not from Sussex.'

'It may have been brought in by the storm,' I remarked. 'Let's go back to my house and I will tell you the experience of a person who met with the same tragedy, but lived to tell about it.'

On reaching the house, we found that Murdoch had recovered enough to sit up. He was dazed and every now and then he was shaken by a wave of pain. He explained that he had no idea about what had happened, except that terrific

This is
Out of Doors

pain had suddenly shot through him and that it had taken all his strength to reach the bank.

I took out the book I had taken from my attic. 'This is *Out of Doors*, by the famous observer, J. G. Wood. Wood himself very nearly died from contact with this creature, so he wrote it with full knowledge. *Cyanea capillata* is its full name and he can be as dangerous to life—and far more painful than the bite of the cobra.'

'He goes on to tell of his own encounter when swimming off the coast of Kent. He found that the creature radiated almost invisible filaments to the distance of fifty feet and that anyone within that distance was in danger of death. The multiple threads caused light scarlet lines upon the skin, which on closer examination resolved into minute dots.

'The local pain was, as he explains, the least part of the extreme trauma. It nearly killed him. He says that he could hardly recognize himself afterwards, so white, wrinkled and shriveled was his face. He drank a full bottle of brandy and it helped save his life. I will leave the book with you, Inspector, and undoubtedly it explains the tragedy of poor McPherson.'

'It also sets me free,' remarked Ian Murdoch with a wry smile. 'I do not blame any of you, for your suspicions were natural. I feel that I have only cleared myself by sharing the fate of my late friend.'

'No, Mr Murdoch. I was already on the trail and if I had gone as early as I intended, I could have saved you from the terrible experience.'

'But how did you know, Mr Holmes?'

'I am an avid reader with a strong memory for small things. That phrase "The Lion's Mane" stuck in my mind. I knew that I had seen it somewhere. You have seen that it does describe the creature. It must have been floating when McPherson saw it and this phrase was the only one by which he could convey to us the reason for his death.'

'Then I am cleared,' said Murdoch. 'There are one or two explanations that are necessary, for I know the direction of your investigations. It is true that I loved this lady, but ever since she chose McPherson, my only wish was to see her happy. I often carried their messages and it was because I was in their confidence that I hurried to tell her of my friend's death. She did not tell you about all this fearing that you might not approve and consequently I might suffer. Allow me to leave now, for I need rest.'

Stackhurst held out his hand.

'Our nerves have been high strung,' he said. 'Forgive what is past, Murdoch. We shall understand each other better in the future.'

They went out together with their arms linked in friendly fashion.

The Adventure of the Mazarin Stone

Arthur Conan Doyle

Dr Watson was happy to be back in the study room of the first floor in Baker Street which had been the starting point of so many remarkable adventures. He looked around him and saw everything unchanged. Finally, his eyes came round to the fresh and smiling face of Billy, the young but very wise and tactful page, who had helped a little to fill up the gap of loneliness and isolation which surrounded the figure of the great detective.

'It all seems very unchanged, Billy. You don't change either. I hope the same can be said of him?'

Billy glanced with some concern at the closed door of the bedroom.

'I think he's in bed and asleep,' he said.

Dr Watson was not surprised at the idea, though it was seven in the evening of a lovely summer day, as he was familiar with his old friend's habit.

'That means a case, I suppose?'

'Yes, sir, he is very hard at it just now. I'm frightened for his health. He gets paler and thinner, and he eats nothing. "When will you be pleased to dine, Mr Holmes?" Mrs Hudson asked. "Seven-thirty, the day after tomorrow," said he. You know his way when he is keen on a case.'

'Yes Billy, I know.'

'He's following someone. Yesterday he was out as a workman looking for a job, Today he was an old woman. Fairly took me in, he did, and I ought to know his ways by now.'

Billy pointed with a grin to a very baggy umbrella which leaned against the sofa.

'That's part of the old woman's outfit,' he said.

'But what is it all about?'

Billy said in a low voice, 'It's the case of the Crown Diamond.'

'What—the hundred-thousand-pound burglary?'

'Yes, sir, we had the Prime Minister and the Home Secretary both sitting on that very sofa. Mr Holmes was very nice to them. He promised them he would do all he could. Then there is Lord Cantlemere.'

'Ah!'

'Yes, sir, you know what that means. I can get along with the Prime Minister, and I've nothing against the Home Secretary, who seemed a civil obliging sort of man, but I can't stand his Lordship. Neither can Mr Holmes, sir. You see, he doesn't believe in Mr Holmes and he was against employing him. He'd rather he failed.'

'Well, we'll hope he won't fail and that Lord Cantlemere will be proved wrong. What is that curtain for across the window?'

'Mr Holmes had it put up there three days ago. We've got something funny behind it.'

When Billy drew away the drapery, Dr Watson could not restrain a cry of amazement. There was a facsimile of his old friend, dressing gown and all, the face turned three-quarters towards the window and downwards, as though reading an invisible book, while the body was sunk deep in an armchair. Billy detached the head and held it in the air.

'We put it at different angles, so that it may seem more life like. I wouldn't dare touch it if the blinds were not down. But when it's up you can see this from across the way.'

Billy drew the window curtains apart and looked out into the street.

'There are folks who watch us from the distance. I can see a fellow now at the window. Have a look for yourself.'

Watson had taken a step forward when the bedroom door opened and the long thin form of Holmes emerged. His face pale and drawn, but his step and bearing as active as ever. Immediately he was at the window and drew the blind once more.

'That will do, Billy,' said he. 'You were in danger of your life then, my boy, and I can't do without you just yet. Well, Watson, it is good to see you in your old quarters once again. You come at a critical moment.'

'So I gather.'

'You can go, Billy. That boy is a problem, Watson. How far am I justified in allowing him to be in danger?'

'Danger of what, Holmes?'

'Of sudden death. I'm expecting something this evening.'

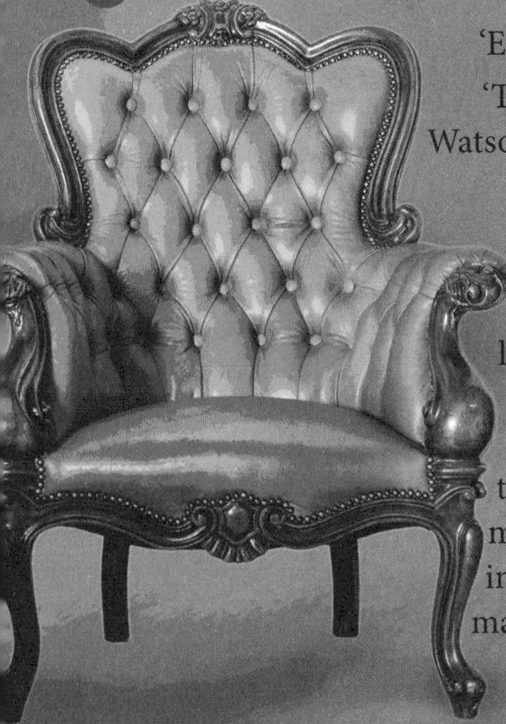

'Expecting what?'

'To be murdered, Watson.'

'No, no, you are joking, Holmes!'

'Even my limited sense of humour could evolve a better joke than that. But we may be comfortable in the meantime, may we not? Is alcohol permitted? The gasogene and cigars are in the old place. Let me see you once more in the customary armchair. You have not, I hope, learned to despise my pipe and my tobacco? It has to take the place of food these days.'

'But why not eat?'

'Because the faculties become refined when you starve them. Why, surely, as a doctor, my dear Watson, you must admit that what your digestion gains in the way of blood supply is so much lost to the brain. I am a brain, Watson. The rest of me is a mere appendix. Therefore, it is the brain I must consider.'

'But this danger, Holmes?'

'Ah, yes, in case it should come of, it would perhaps be as well that you should burden your memory with the name and address of the murderer. You can give it to Scotland Yard, with my love and a parting blessing. Sylvius is the name—Count Negretto Sylvius. Write it down, man, write it down! 136 Moorside Gardens, NW. Got it?'

Watson knew only too well the immense risks taken by Holmes, so he rose to the occasion.

'Count me in, Holmes I have nothing to do for a day or two.'

'Your morals don't improve, Watson. You have added umbrella to your other vices. You bear every sign of the busy medical man, with calls on him every hour.'

'Not such important ones. But can't you have this fellow arrested?'

'Yes, Watson, I could. That's what worries him so.'

'But why don't you?'

'Because I don't know where the diamond is.'

'Ah! Billy told me—the missing Crown Jewel!'

'Yes, the great yellow Mazarin stone. I have cast my net and I have my fish. But I have not got the stone. What is the use of taking them? We can make the world a better place by laying them by the heels. But that is not what I am out for. It's the stone I want.'

'And is Count Sylvius one of your fish?'

'Yes, he's a shark. He bites. The other is Sam Merton, the boxer. Not a bad fellow, Sam, but the Count has used him. Sam's not a shark. He is a great big silly bull-headed fellow. But he is flopping about in my net all the same.'

'Where is this Count Sylvius?'

'I've been at his very elbow all the morning. You've seen me as an old lady, Watson. He actually picked up my parasol for me once.'

"By your leave, madame," said he. 'Half-Italian, you know, and with the Southern graces of manner when in the mood, but a devil incarnate in the other mood. Life is full of whimsical happenings, Watson.'

'It might have been tragedy.'

'Well perhaps it might. I followed him to old Straubenzee's workshop in the Minories, Straubenzee made the air gun. It is at the opposite window at the present moment. The dummy may get a bullet through its beautiful head at any moment.'

'Ah,' Billy what is it?'

The boy came with a card upon a tray.

'The man himself! I had hardly expected this. This is a proof that he feels my toe very close behind his heel.'

'Send for the police.'

'I probably shall. But not just yet. Would you glance carefully out of the window, Watson, and see if anyone is hanging about in the street?'

Watson looked warily round the edge of the curtain.

'Yes, there is one rough fellow near the door.'

'That will be Sam Merton—the faithful but rather silly Sam. Where is this gentleman, Billy?'

'In the waiting room, sir.'

'Show him up when I ring.'

'Yes, sir.'

'If I am not in the room, show him in all the same.'

'Yes, sir.'

Watson waited until the door was closed, and then he turned earnestly to his companion.

'Look here, Holmes, this is simply impossible. This is a desperate man, who sticks at nothing. He may have come to murder you.'

'I should not be surprised.'

'I insist upon staying with you.'

'You would be horribly in the way.'

'In his way?'

'No, my dear fellow—in my way.'

'Well, I can't possibly leave you.'

'Yes, you can, Watson. And you will, for you have never failed to play the game. I am sure you will play it to the end. This man has come for his own purpose, but he may stay for mine.'

Holmes took out his notebook and scribbled a few lines.

'Take a cab to Scotland Yard and give this to Youghal of the CID. Come back with the police. The fellow's arrest will follow.'

'I'll do that with joy.'

'Before you return I may have just time enough to find out where the stone is.'

He touched the bell.

'I think we will go out through the bedroom. This second exit is exceedingly useful. I rather want to see my shark without his seeing me, and I have, as you will remember, my own way of doing it.'

It was, therefore, an empty room into which Billy, a minute later, ushered Count Sylvius. The famous game-shot, sportsman, and man-about-town was a big swarthy fellow, with a formidable dark moustache shading a cruel thin-lipped mouth, and surmounted by a long curved nose like the beak of an eagle. He was well-dressed, but his brilliant necktie, shining pin, and glittering rings were flamboyant in their effect. As the door closed behind him he looked round him with fierce startled eyes, like one who suspects a trap at every turn. Then he gave a violent start as he saw the impassive head and the collar of the dressing gown which projected above the armchair in the window. At first his expression was one of pure amazement. Then the light of a horrible hope gleamed in his dark murderous eyes. He took one more glance around to see that there were no witnesses, and then, on tiptoe, his thick stick half raised, he approached the silent figure. He was crouching for his final spring and blow when a cool sardonic voice greeted him from the open bedroom door:

'Don't break it, Count! Don't break it!'

The assassin staggered back, amazement in his convulsed face. For an instant he half raised his loaded cane once more, as if he would turn his violence from the effigy to the original, but there was something in that steady grey eye and mocking smile which caused his hand to sink to his side.

'It's a pretty little thing,' said Holmes, advancing towards the image. 'Tavernier, the French modeller, made it. He is as good at waxworks as your friend Straubenzee is at air-guns.'

'Air-guns, sir! What do you mean?'

'Put your hat and stick on the side table. Thank you! Pray take a seat. Would you care to put your revolver out also? Oh, very good, if you prefer to sit upon it. Your visit is really most opportune, for I wanted badly to have a few minutes' chat with you.'

The Count scowled, with heavy threatening eyebrows.

'I, too, wished to have some words with you, Holmes. That is why I am here. I won't deny that I intended to assault you just now.'

Holmes swung his leg on the edge of the table.

'I rather gathered that you had some idea of the sort in your head,' said he. 'But why these personal attentions?'

'Because you have gone out of your way to annoy me. Because you have put your creatures upon my track.'

'My creatures! I assure you no!'

'Nonsense! I have had them followed. Two can play at that game, Holmes.'

'It is a small point, Count Sylvius, but perhaps you would kindly give me my prefix when you address me. You can understand that, with my routine of work, I should find myself on familiar terms with half the rogues' gallery, and you will agree that exceptions are invidious.'

'Well, Mr Holmes, then.'

'Excellent! But I assure you, you are mistaken about my alleged agents.'

Count Sylvius laughed contemptuously.

'Other people can observe as well as you. Yesterday there was an old sporting man. Today it was an elderly woman. They held me in view all day.'

'Really, sir, you compliment me. Old Baron Dowson said the night before he was hanged that in my case what the law had gained the stage had lost. And now you give my little impersonations your kindly praise?'

'It was you—you yourself?'

Holmes shrugged his shoulders.

'You can see in the corner the umbrella which you so politely handed to me in the Minories before you began to suspect.'

'If I had known, you might never—'

'Have seen this humble home again. I was well aware of it. We all have neglected opportunities to deplore. As it happens, you did not know, so here we are!'

The Count's knotted brows gathered more heavily over his menacing eyes.

'What you say only makes the matter worse. It was not your agents but your play-acting, busybody self! You admit that you have dogged me. Why?'

'Come now, Count. You used to shoot lions in Algeria.'

'Well?'

'But why?'

'Why? The sport—the excitement—the danger!'

'And, no doubt, to free the country from a pest?'

'Exactly!'

'My reasons in a nutshell!'

The Count sprang to his feet, and his hand involuntarily moved back to his hip pocket.

'Sit down, sir, sit down! There was another, more practical, reason. I want that yellow diamond!'

Count Sylvius lay back in his chair with an evil smile.

'Upon my word!' said he.

'You knew that I was after you for that. The real reason why you are here tonight is to find out how much I know about the matter and how far my removal is absolutely essential. Well, I should say that, from your point of view, it is absolutely essential, for I know all about it, save only one thing, which you are about to tell me.'

'Oh, indeed! And pray, what is this missing fact?'

'Where the Crown diamond now is.'

The Count looked sharply at his companion.

'Oh, you want to know that, do you? How the devil should I be

able to tell you where it is?'

'You can, and you will.'

'Indeed!'

'You can't bluff me, Count Sylvius.'

Holmes's eyes, as he gazed at him, contracted and lightened until they were like two menacing points of steel.

'You are absolute plate-glass. I see to the very back of your mind.'

'Then, of course, you see where the diamond is!'

Holmes clapped his hands with amusement, and then pointed a finger mockingly.

'Then you do know. You have admitted it!'

'I admit nothing.'

'Now, Count, if you will be reasonable we can do business. If not, you will get hurt.'

Count Sylvius threw up his eyes to the ceiling.

'And you talk about bluff!' said he.

Holmes looked at him thoughtfully like a master chess player who meditated his crowning move.

Then he threw open the table drawer and drew out a squat notebook.

'Do you know what I keep in this book?'

'No, sir, I do not!'

'You!'

'Me!'

'Yes, sir, you! You are all here—every action of your vile and dangerous life.'

'Damn you, Holmes!' cried the Count with blazing eyes. 'There are limits to my patience!'

'It's all here, Count. The real facts as to the death of old Mrs Harold, who left you the Blymer estate, which you so rapidly gambled away.'

'You are dreaming!'

'And the complete life history of Miss Minnie Warrender.'

'Tut! You will make nothing of that!'

'Plenty more here, Count. Here is the robbery in the train deluxe to the Riviera on 13 February 1892. Here is the forged check in the same year on the Credit Lyonnais.'

'No, you're wrong there.'

'Then I am right on the others! Now, Count, you are a card player. When the other fellow has all the trumps, it saves time to throw down your hand.'

'What has all this talk to do with the jewel of which you spoke?'

'Gently, Count. Restrain that eager mind! Let me get to the points in my own dull fashion. I have all this against you but, above all, I have a clear case against both you and your fighting bully in the case of the Crown diamond.'

'Indeed!'

'I have the cabman who took you to Whitehall and the cabman who brought you away. I have the commissionaire who saw you near the case. I have Ikey Sanders, who refused to cut it up for you. Ikey has peached, and the game is up.'

The veins stood out on the Count's forehead.

His dark hairy hands were clenched in a convulsion of restrained emotion. He tried to speak, but the words would not shape themselves.

'That's the hand I play from,' said Holmes. 'I put it all upon the table. But one card is missing. It's the king of diamonds. I don't know where the stone is.'

'You never shall know.'

'No? Now, be reasonable, Count. Consider the situation. You are going to be locked up for twenty years. So is Sam Merton. What good are you going to get out of your diamond? None in the world. But if you hand it over—well, I'll compound a felony. We don't want you or Sam. We want the stone. Give that up, and so far as I am concerned you can go free so long as you behave yourself in the future. If you make another slip—well, it will be the last. But this time my commission is to get the stone, not you.'

'But if I refuse?'

'Why, then—alas!—it must be you and not the stone.'

Billy had appeared in answer to a ring.

'I think, Count, that it would be as well to have your friend Sam at this conference. After all, his interests should be represented. Billy, you will see a large and ugly gentleman outside the front door. Ask him to come up.'

'If he won't come, sir?'

'No violence, Billy. Don't be rough with him. If you tell him that Count Sylvius wants him he will certainly come.'

'What are you going to do now?' asked the Count as Billy disappeared.

'My friend Watson was with me just now. I told him that I had a shark and a fish in my net; now I am drawing the net and up they come together.'

The Count had risen from his chair, and his hand was behind his back. Holmes held something half protruding from the pocket of his dressing gown.

'You won't die in your bed, Holmes.'

'I have often had the same idea. Does it matter very much? After all, Count, your own exit is more likely to be perpendicular than horizontal. But these anticipations of the future are morbid. Why not give ourselves up to the unrestrained enjoyment of the present?'

A sudden wildbeast light sprang up in the dark menacing eyes of the master criminal. Holmes's figure seemed to grow taller as he grew tense and ready.

'It is no use your fingering your revolver, my friend,' he said in a quiet voice. 'You know perfectly well that you dare not use it, even if I gave you time to draw it. Nasty noisy things, revolvers, Count. Better stick to air-guns. Ah! I think I hear the fairy footstep of your estimable partner. Good day, Mr Merton. Rather dull in the street, is it not?'

The prize-fighter, a heavily built young man with a stupid, obstinate, slab-sided face, stood awkwardly at the door, looking about him with a puzzled expression. Holmes's debonair manner was a new experience, and though he vaguely felt that it was hostile, he did not know how to counter it. He turned to his more astute comrade for help.

'What's the game now, Count? What's this fellow want? What's up?' His voice was deep and raucous.

The Count shrugged his shoulders, and it was Holmes who answered.

'If I may put it briefly, Mr Merton, I should say it was all up.'

The boxer still addressed his remarks to his associate.

'Is he trying to be funny, or what? I'm not in the funny mood myself.'

'No, I expect not,' said Holmes. 'I think I can promise you that you will feel even less humorous as the evening advances. Now, look here, Count Sylvius. I'm a busy man and I can't waste time. I'm going into that bedroom. Pray make yourselves quite at home in my absence. You can explain to your friend how the matter lies without the restraint of my presence. I shall try over the Hoffman "Barcarole" upon my violin. In five minutes I shall return for your final answer. You quite grasp the alternative, do you not? Shall we take you, or shall we have the stone?'

Holmes withdrew, picking up his violin from the corner as he passed. A few moments later the long-drawn, wailing notes of that most haunting of tunes came faintly through the closed door of the bedroom.

'What is it, then?' asked Merton anxiously as his companion turned to him.

'Does he know about the stone?'

'He knows a damned sight too much about it. I'm not sure that he doesn't know all about it.'

'Good Lord!'

The boxer's sallow face turned a shade whiter.

'Ikey Sanders has split on us.'

'He has, has he? I'll do him down a thick 'un for that if I swing for it.'

'That won't help us much. We've got to make up our minds what to do.'

'Half a moment,' said the boxer, looking suspiciously at the bedroom door. 'He needs to be watched. I suppose he's not listening?'

'How can he be listening with that music going?'

'That's right. Maybe somebody's behind a curtain. Too many curtains in this room!'

As he looked round he suddenly saw for the first time the effigy in the window, and stood staring and pointing, too amazed for words.

'Tut! It's only a dummy,' said the Count.

'A fake, is it? Well, strike me! Madame Tussaud isn't in it. It's the living spit of him, gown and all. But them curtains, Count!'

'Oh, confound the curtains! We are wasting our time, and there is none too much. He can lag us over this stone.'

'The briefest he can!'

'But he'll let us slip if we only tell him where the swag is.'

'What! Give it up? Give up a hundred thousand quid?'

'It's one or the other.'

Merton scratched his short-cropped head.

'He's alone in there. Let's do him in. If his light were out we should have nothing to fear.'

The Count shook his head.

'He is armed and ready. If we shot him we could hardly get away in a place like this. Besides, it's likely enough that the police know whatever evidence he has got. Hello! What was that?'

There was a vague sound which seemed to come from the window. Both men sprang round, but all was quiet. Save for the one strange figure seated in the chair, the room was certainly empty.

'Something in the street,' said Merton. 'Now look here, you've got the brains. Surely you can think a way out of it. If slugging is no use then it's up to you.'

'I've fooled better men than he,' the Count answered.

'The stone is here in my secret pocket. I take no chances leaving it about. It can be out of England tonight and cut into four pieces in Amsterdam before Sunday. He knows nothing of Van Seddar.'

'I thought Van Seddar was going next week.'

'He was. But now he must get off by the next boat. One or other of us must slip round with the stone to Lime Street and tell him.'

'But the false bottom ain't ready.'

'Well, he must take it as it is and chance it. There's not a moment to lose.'

Again, with the sense of danger which becomes an instinct with the sportsman, he paused and looked hard at the window. Yes, it was surely from the street that the faint sound had come.

'As to Holmes,' he continued, 'we can fool him easily enough. You see, the damned fool won't arrest us if he can get the stone. Well, we'll promise him the stone. We'll put him on the wrong track about it, and before he finds that it is the wrong track it will be in Holland and we out of the country.'

'That sounds good to me!' cried Sam Merton with a grin.

'You go on and tell the Dutchman to get a move on him. I'll see this sucker and fill him up with a bogus confession. I'll tell him that the stone is in Liverpool. Confound that whining music; it gets on my nerves! By the time he finds it isn't in Liverpool it will be in quarters and we on the blue water. Come back here, out of a line with that keyhole. Here is the stone.'

'I wonder you dare carry it.'

'Where could I have it safer? If we could take

it out of Whitehall someone else could surely take it out of my lodgings.'

'Let's have a look at it.'

Count Sylvius cast a somewhat unflattering glance at his associate and disregarded the unwashed hand which was extended towards him.

'What—do you think I'm going to snatch it off you? See here, mister, I'm getting a bit tired of your ways.'

'Well, well, no offence, Sam. We can't afford to quarrel. Come over to the window if you want to see the beauty properly. Now hold it to the light!'

'Here!'

'Thank you!'

With a single spring Holmes had leaped from the dummy's chair and had grasped the precious jewel. He held it now in one hand, while his other pointed a revolver at the Count's head. The two villains staggered back in utter amazement. Before they had recovered Holmes had pressed the electric bell.

'No violence, gentlemen—no violence, I beg of you! Consider the furniture! It must be very clear to you that your position is an impossible one. The police are waiting below.'

The Count's bewilderment overmastered his rage and fear.

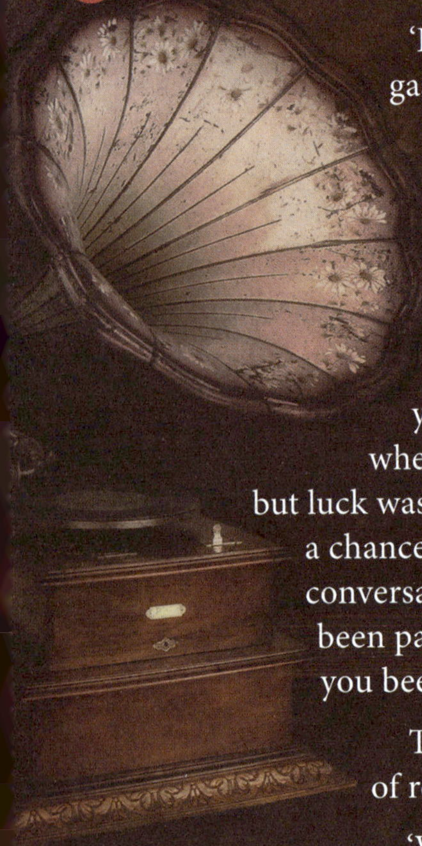

'But how the deuce—?' he gasped.

'Your surprise is very natural. You are not aware that a second door from my bedroom leads behind that curtain. I fancied that you must have heard me when I displaced the figure, but luck was on my side. It gave me a chance of listening to your racy conversation which would have been painfully constrained had you been aware of my presence.'

The Count gave a gesture of resignation.

'We give you best, Holmes. I believe you are the devil himself.'

'Not far from him, at any rate,' Holmes answered with a polite smile.

Sam Merton's slow intellect had only gradually comprehended the situation. Now, as the sound of heavy steps came from the stairs outside, he broke silence at last.

'A fair cop!' said he. 'But, I say, what about that bloomin' fiddle! I hear it yet.'

'Tut, tut!' Holmes answered. 'You are perfectly right. Let it play! These modern gramophones are a remarkable invention.'

There was an inrush of police, the handcuffs clicked and the criminals were led to the waiting cab. Watson lingered with Holmes, congratulating him upon this fresh leaf added to his laurels.

Once more their conversation was interrupted by the calm Billy with his card-tray.

'Lord Cantlemere, sir.'

'Show him up, Billy. This is the eminent peer who represents the very highest interests,' said Holmes. 'He is an excellent and loyal person, but rather of the old regime. Shall we make him unbend? Dare we venture upon a slight liberty? He knows, we may conjecture, nothing of what has occurred.'

The door opened to admit a thin, austere figure with a hatchet face and drooping mid-Victorian whiskers of a glossy blackness which hardly corresponded with the rounded shoulders and feeble gait. Holmes advanced affably, and shook an unresponsive hand.

'How do you do, Lord Cantlemere? It is chilly for the time of year, but rather warm indoors. May I take your overcoat?'

'No, I thank you; I will not take it off.'

Holmes laid his hand insistently upon the sleeve.

'Pray allow me! My friend Dr Watson would assure you that these changes of temperature are most tempting.'

His Lordship shook himself free with some impatience.

'I am quite comfortable, sir. I have no need to stay. I have simply looked in to know how your self-appointed task was progressing.'

'It is difficult—very difficult.'

'I feared that you would find it so.'

There was a distinct sneer in the old courtier's words and manner.

'Every man finds his limitations, Mr Holmes, but at least it cures us of the weakness of self-satisfaction.'

'Yes, sir, I have been much confused.'

'No doubt.'

'Especially upon one point. Possibly you could help me upon it?'

'You apply for my advice rather late in the day. I thought that you had your own all-sufficient methods. Still, I am ready to help you.'

'You see, Lord Cantlemere, we can no doubt frame a case against the actual thieves.'

'When you have caught them.'

'Exactly. But the question is—how shall we proceed against the receiver?'

'Is this not rather premature?'

'It is as well to have our plans ready. Now, what would you regard as final evidence against the receiver?'

'The actual possession of the stone.'

'You would arrest him upon that?'

'Most undoubtedly.'

Holmes seldom laughed, but he got as near it as his old friend Watson could remember.

'In that case, my dear sir, I shall be under the painful necessity of advising your arrest.'

Lord Cantlemere was very angry. Some of the ancient fires flickered up into his sallow cheeks.

'You take a great liberty, Mr Holmes. In fifty years of official life I cannot recall such a case. I am a busy man, sir, engaged upon important affairs, and I have no time or taste for foolish jokes. I may tell you frankly, sir, that I have never been a believer in your powers, and that I have always been of the opinion that the matter was far safer in the hands of the regular police force. Your conduct confirms all my conclusions. I have the honour, sir, to wish you good-evening.'

Holmes had swiftly changed his position and was between the peer and the door.

'One moment, sir,' said he. 'To actually go off with the Mazarin stone would be a more serious offence than to be found in temporary possession of it.'

'Sir, this is intolerable! Let me pass.'

'Put your hand in the right-hand pocket of your overcoat.'

'What do you mean, sir?'

'Come—come, do what I ask.'

An instant later the amazed peer was standing, blinking and stammering, with the great yellow stone on his shaking palm.

'What! What! How is this, Mr Holmes?'

'Too bad, Lord Cantlemere, too bad!' cried Holmes. 'My old friend here will tell you that I have an impish habit of practical joking. Also that I can never resist a dramatic situation. I took the liberty—the very great liberty, I admit—of putting the stone into your pocket at the beginning of our interview.'

The old peer stared from the stone to the smiling face before him.

'Sir, I am lost. But—yes—it is indeed the Mazarin stone. We are greatly your debtors, Mr Holmes. Your sense of humour may, as you admit, be somewhat perverted, and its exhibition remarkably untimely, but at least I withdraw any reflection I have made upon your amazing professional powers. But how—'

'The case is but half-finished; the details can wait. No doubt, Lord Cantlemere, your pleasure in telling of this successful result in the exalted circle to which you return will be some small atonement for my practical joke. Billy, you will show his Lordship out, and tell Mrs Hudson that I should be glad if she would send up dinner for two as soon as possible.'

Other Titles in the Series

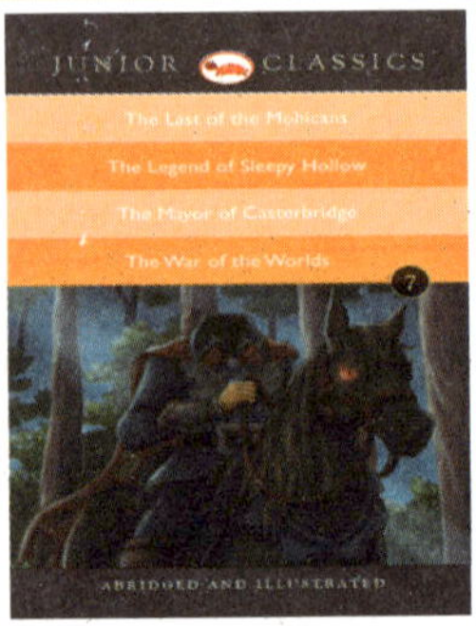

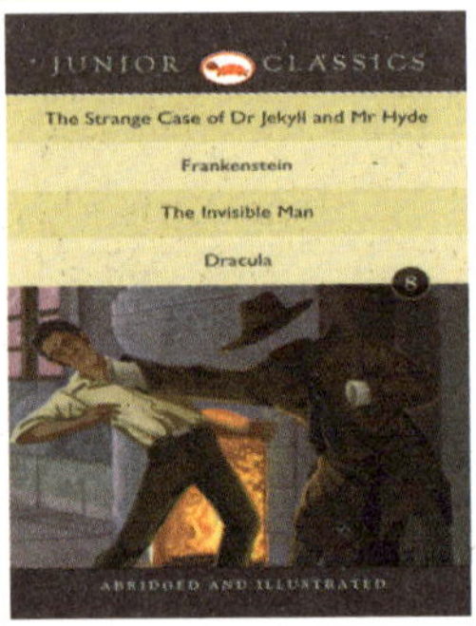